BETWEEN THE PAGES

SAMANTHA GOLLAKNER

ISBN: 978-0-578-54401-4

CHAPTER ONE:

The dark clouds that have been rolling over the skyline taunt me as I sit in the corner bar, not far from my home. I can feel the tips of my fingers running along the chipped rim of my now empty glass.

It does not take long for the woman behind the counter to notice.

She flashes me a fast grin. She leans her torso forward allowing the fair, bare skin showing from underneath her top to press against the barrier between us.

She speaks in a comforting sway, "Another fireball?"

The lingering taste of cinnamon remains fresh on my tongue as I nod my head once in approval.

My focus becomes suddenly shot to my left as I hear the slurring stroll of an unknown male blaring through my mind, "Ya know, kid. Whatever you are running from, you aren't going to get far if you hide in that bottle."

I allow my vision to follow the gesture of his right, index finger as he aims it in a shaken sway towards my freshly filled shot glass.

I clasp my open palm around the chilled holder, admiring the caramel-colored liquid inside, "Well, tonight we are going to at least give it a try."

The sound of the glass smashing into the wooden surface is drowned out by the man's raspy laughter.

I feel the warmth of his large, right hand rest against my upper back, "I like you. What's your name?"

The gentle tug of a slight smile creeps along my lips, "Sam. You?"

I stare into the vast void of his glossy, pale blue eyes, "Most people call me Steven, but I prefer Steve."

The weight of my head pulls down slightly in a small motion of understanding.

The break of silence between us is caused by his harsh words, "What about you? Is Sam, short for anything?"

I drop my gaze towards the ground, slightly shrugging my shoulders.

I catch his reaction out of the corner of my left eye, watching his vision widen slightly as if in a surprised manner.

I allow the palm of my right hand to knock against the top of the counter, gathering the bartender's attention, "I'll have another one."

I begin pushing the weight of my figure into a forwards motion, turning towards Steve, "I'm going to the bathroom. I'll be right back."

Before walking too far away, I turn my head gently towards him, speaking in a playful manner, "Don't steal my drink while I am gone."

The walk to the back of the bar is long and slow.

My main focus has shifted from having to get out of the crowd for a moment to breathe, onto trying to regain control of my swaying form, that nearly stumbles into the wall of the hall as I try to get to the facilities.

Finally, I feel my body collapse onto the front of the sink as I attempt to get a clearer view of my current appearance.

My blurred vision shoots back the reflection of my flushed, pale skin. I can see beads of sweat lining the structure of my face. I notice that my hair is in a messy, whirl of dark brown strands, spiked up along the top of my head. I feel the movement of my left fingertips grip the sink as anxiety begins to rise in my body from being face to face with the unknown entity in the mirror.

I release a long sigh giving myself a sense of grounding by focusing on my hazy, blue eyes. The only thing that I still recognize. My soul is being weighed down by a deep sadness, one of which I find myself constantly trying to escape from.

I quickly turn on the facet allowing a stream of cool water to rinse over the black ink stains of a sun and moon that cover the outer portions of my hands.

I depart the washroom with a quickened pace giving my vision free range to sweep the area.

My attention falls upon Steve. He is an older gentleman, his tan skin is mostly hidden under the attire of a matching, black suit and tie. The strands of his jet-black hair remain held in a tight placement by the gel that I can see reflecting from the above lighting. The leather holder of a light brown, messenger bag is slung over the back of his chair.

I once again slide into the wooden stool, hoping to quickly down my next shot of medicine.

My mind begins to glide through the vortex of my dream, *'Every night, it is the same. The girl who hides behind my wildest imagination, sitting alongside me on a concrete step of an unknown house. I can see the top of her pecan, misty hair, sprouting from a darker tint of strands. The warmth of her soul is radiating through the pores of her facial structure as her head rests gently upon my shoulder. I inhale the lingering smell of freshly brewed coffee, swirling with the wind in an upwards movement towards my brain. My vision scans the area, seeing that just up ahead, to the left is a two-pronged street sign with a metal stake to hold it in place. The base of the background is a brighter green in color with bold, white letters informing me that we are on 28th and Lincoln.'*

The crackle of Steve's voice burns the back of my mind, pulling me out of the realm of my thoughts.

I soon find that his voice is harsher than the liquor, "What do you do for a living?"

I use my right hand to motion for the bartender to give me another round, "I am a writer, you?"

The harshness of his deepened laugh rings through my soul, "That explains the drinking. I am a messenger."

I feel the weight of my right eyebrow raise slightly, "Like a mail man or what?"

He flashes me a fast grin while holding a glance at his beer in a tinted bottle, "No, not a mail man. So, are you married?"

A gust of air is pushed from my lungs, "No, are you?"

His reply is faster than I expected, "Why not?"

I cross the structure of my arms in a tight hold over my chest, "I do not know. I guess, I just never found the right girl. Isn't that what everyone says?"

I see the silent humor light up his vision, "Ah, you will find her, don't worry. Anyway, who knows? Maybe, she is in the next chapter of your life."

I choke on the gulp of liquid heat, "The perfect girl just does not exist, but I guess you never really know, do you?"

A long pause grows between us.

His voice blares against me without warning in an upbeat manner, "Hey, I got an idea. Why don't you write about her?"

I tilt my head slightly to the right in misunderstanding, "I am sorry, write about who?"

He presses his point with a serious flick of the tongue, "The perfect girl for you. Maybe, she will read your book and come find you!"

I swish the structure of my lips to the left side of my mouth as I think over the idea for a moment, "I don't know, man. I really do not think it would work. Thank you, for the advice though. I appreciate it."

He pulls his figure into a full stance, reaching into his right, back pants pocket to retrieve his cracked, tan, leather wallet, "Just think about it. Even if she doesn't come find you, at least you have the chance to know what you are looking for. It might save you a lot of trouble in the future."

His voice becomes overtaken by a stern vibe, turning towards the barkeep, "I am going to cover Sam's, too."

The woman smiles giving him a slight nod.

She steadies her dominate hand as she pours me my last drink of the night, shot number eight. I down it quickly. I turn my head to the left attempting to thank Steve, but he is nowhere in sight.

My vision becomes glued to the dark tan, leather binding of a book that has been left behind on the counter, where Steve was sitting only moments before.

I feel the movement of my right hand extend away from my form as I reach for the hunk of paper. The cover feels cool under the heat radiating from my flesh. My vision brushes along a title, engraved in gold ink that reads, *FATE*.

I smirk to myself as I thumb through the pages, finding that every single one of them are blank.

On the opening page, something in the shade of a light blue catches my attention.

I allow its pull to grab a hold of me as I can feel it silently demanding my focus, standing out against the cream-colored paper.

I scan the sloppy cursive, scrolled along the sticky note,

'Sam. Please, accept this book.

Maybe, you will write the best story yet in it.

Best of luck,

Steven.'

The weight of my head pulls into a slow shake as I think to myself, *'Well, it's not the weirdest gift I've ever been given at a bar. Who knows? Maybe, he is right. I will give it a shot, it might spark some good ideas.'*

CHAPTER TWO:

I drag myself out of the bar and into the crisp, night air.

My internal compass begins to guide me back towards my apartment.

With my new journal tucked safely away, under my right arm, I allow myself to get lost in thoughts about my life. With me knowing that my body is now set on autopilot, I make it to the front door of my house in what feels to me as mere seconds.

My right fingers twist and turn in various directions as I fumble with placing the correct key into the slot on the lock. A flash of relief floods my chest, hearing the bolt unlatch from the frame. While pushing the door in, I am bombarded by the stale oxygen, recycling from the air conditioning unit. With it, comes the delicate fragrance of a calming, ocean breeze from my go-to air cleanser.

I am greeted by the bare setting of white walls running into sand colored carpeting that is mostly covered by a minimal amount of randomly picked pieces of furniture.

I would love to say that this is my home, but I think the term *house* is more fitting. I never really had a place I could call home, a place I felt content or comfortable, nevertheless—vulnerable.

This place has just the basics, I do not like the look of clutter.

I always thought this was much more appealing, but my drunken mind does not approve of the current non-matching decor.

I sigh gently through the crack of my lips.

My weight is being guided towards the kitchen. I walk by my circular, glass table with a silver, metal frame that holds it together. My left hand releases the grip on the book, letting it rest on top. I hear the glass settling under the weight of the notepad.

While it is fading from my hearing, I begin to search for items that will help me settle in for the night.

I waste no time grabbing a fresh bottle of vodka from my collection. A frozen pack of menthol cigarettes from the freezer and a black inked pen that I spotted laying on the countertop by the sink when I first walked into this dwelling.

The wobbly structure of my form guides me to the chair at the head of the table, placing my back towards the exit and all windows of the outdoor surroundings. I find it is easiest for me to work without the chance of a distraction. My weight sinks into the metal structure. I feel the small release of air leave the black leather cushion underneath me.

I lay out my gathered items, opening the bottle. I allow my thirst to become drier as I inhale a big swig of burning liquid.

My left hand opens the book, I scan the structure of the first page. While my mind is focusing on what to write, my hands are set and ready, captivated by the task of retrieving a stick of tobacco from the paper pack.

The yellow filter sits loosely between my lips. My taste buds flush with the cooling effect of menthol as I inhale a slow, deep breath. I feel the intake of a smooth drag while the light from the crackling flame dies slowly from the metal casing of my lighter.

I push the tip of my pen down causing it to scroll effortlessly along the paper's surface.

She is nothing more than a mere thought. Her life exists only inside of the brightest corners of my mind. Some days, I find myself sleeping away the sun's gift of a new day, wishing to spend as much time with her as possible, but only being able to spot her in the darkness that lays behind my closed eyes, makes a hole break in the center of my chest that I have been trying to fill for as long as I can remember.

When my mind drifts, it never fails to find her. It always starts with her eyes, they melt into my vision, shinning with the different hues of a light brown. Strands of her long, misted hair glide effortlessly against the structure of her chest as she walks in my direction.

She would appear to be heading right towards me. My focus is currently wrapped around her smile. It overtakes the rest of the surroundings, making the whole world seem dull in comparison to her very existence. Something about her, makes me feel like I can finally intake air. Yet, at the same time, her invisible presence in my mind causes my lungs to feel like they are going to explode.

The closer she gets, the faster my heart pounds against the inner lining of my chest. I want to reach out to her, to graze the tips of my fingers gently along the surface of her flawless, olive tainted skin, but I do not move an inch. All I can do is admire her, standing now less than three-feet in front of me. I feel my vision begin to scan her attire of a short, black dress with matching heels. My throat burns with the words building inside of my vocal chamber.

I place the pen down on the glass table, throwing my weight against the backrest of the chair in frustration.

I inhale a long drag of the thinning cigarette, that is currently held between my thumb and index finger.

I growl under my breath, "This is so stupid. I never know what to say to her. She is always in my mind, but it never gets any further than this. It is like something about this woman leaves me at a loss for words."

I shake my head lightly, hoping to clear out my thoughts as I push a long stream of smoke from my lungs. I reach my right hand forward, grabbing the bottle. I hope that it will drown out the block in my mind.

When my eyes graze against the cream-colored page, I freeze to the spot. Something strange has captured my attention, my head tilts to the right as I read the text.

"Maybe, it will be better if I start. How are you? My name is Victoria and yours?"

I strain my eyes allowing them to blink at a rapid movement trying to bring any form of sense to this strange phenomenon.

I run the grooves of my right, index finger over the fresh line of ink staining the page. My pupils widen sharply finding that the scribbles do not smear, and the letters have already soaked into the natural fabric.

I shake my head roughly, throwing back another gulp of the burning juice, "Ah—I see what is happening! It must be the liquor! I had way too much to drink tonight!"

I feel the tugging of a small smile crawling against my mouth, "Well, I did always hear that you are supposed to write drunk. Plus, it is giving me the courage to finally be able to play out my dazing mind with the woman of my dreams. Hell, why not?"

I re-position the weight of my form giving myself full access to the page's view as my shaken, right hand guides the pen back towards the surface.

"Hi. I am well, thanks for asking. How are you? My name is Sam. I cannot believe that I am finally talking to you."

My eyes remain stuck on the page as I see the faint streaks of words beginning to boil to the surface.

Victoria releases a small giggle as the words are transferred to her, "It is nice that we are able to have a chance to speak. I do not know how it is that we have gone all of this time without meeting."

I feel the light tug of a smile running against my lips as I write.

"Maybe, we just weren't supposed to meet until now."

I lift the pen from the page momentarily, when an idea shoots against my thoughts.

"Hey, do you want to have a drink with me?"

A hidden smile runs against her lips, "Yes. That would be nice."

I feel an inhale of relaxation flushing over my brain.

"Ha-ha, okay. Coming right up, ma am."

The smile burning along my lips begins to fade as reality starts to close in on me, reminding my soul that I cannot stay with her for long.

The pen slowly scratches down the next line of action as I scroll in a saddened sway of my wrist.

I push the crystal glass towards Victoria. She reaches her dominate hand to meet me halfway. She grasps it in a delicate sway.

I watch her contently, she uses her left fingertips to clasp around the thin, black straw which I placed inside of the glass. She gives it a small twirl.

Her right shoulder strains in a fast movement allowing the softness of her lips to embrace the edge. She feels the cool drops of vodka and water mixing around inside of her mouth.

I tilt my head to the right trying to piece together what she must look like, right now if she were really in front of me in this moment.

My hand feels as though it cannot write fast enough as a current of excitement fills my form.

"Are you enjoying it?"

The words appear faster than before.

"Yes. It is my favorite drink. How did you know?"

I cannot hold back the slight chuckle that escapes my lips.

"Lucky guess, I suppose."

My eyes scan the area, waiting patiently for a reply.

I feel like an eternity passes before the dark hue stains the surface as she questions me.

I can feel her amusement seeping through the page.

"So, why don't you tell me about yourself?"

I suddenly feel at a loss for words which I find strange. Most people do not carry such an effect on me.

I exhale loudly allowing the humid mist of my breath to nudge against my forearm.

"What do you want to know?"

I feel the anxiety coursing through my right leg causing my foot to tap along the carpet while I wait patiently for her reply.

She tilts her head to the left, "What do you do for a living? We will start with something easy."

I inhale sharply allowing my lungs to indulge on the first drag of my third cigarette since I got home.

The smoke trails in an upwards motion towards my eyes, clouding my vision as I attempt to scribble down my thoughts.

"I am a writer. What about you?"

My mind begins to reel as I hurry to jot down my thoughts before she has a chance to respond.

"Do you want another drink?"

I feel a nervous energy that I am not used to experiencing, trail along the track of my blood.

She shifts in her wooden bar stool allowing her beige nails to clink along the side of the glass.

"I own a salon. And yes, I do."

She pauses slightly, using her right, index finger to try and hide her smile, placing it against her mouth.

"Are you having one as well?"

I nod my head once as I try to retain the information.

My hand begins to shake causing the letters to become blurred.

"That is really cool. Do you like what you do? Yes, I will have another with you."

While I wait for her to give me a line of information, I begin to prepare her a drink.

I gently slide a fresh glass towards her. The clear mixture of liquids sloshes around inside the casing as it comes to a sharp halt against her warm grasp.

The soft crack of her voice comes to life.

"Yes, my daughter does hair, so it works out well. What are you drinking?"

The stinging ping of the bottom of my bottle reconnecting with the glass surface rings through my ears.

I can feel the weight of my stomach drop at the mention of her kids. I see the negativity transfer through the pen, I hope she does not notice.

"Wow, that is really cool. How old is your daughter? Same thing as you, vodka."

She takes a large sip of the drink, it stings the back of her throat on the way down as she thinks her reply over in her mind.

"Yes, it is. She is twenty-two. Good choice on the drink. How many have you had?"

I feel the upper-half of my form sway slightly to the left.

"I have had a fair amount."

I find her question to be amusing. I feel myself wondering, *'Is she asking out of care or other reasons?'*

I attempt to readjust my brain towards the conversation at hand.

"Is she your only child?"

I become mesmerized by the soft marks that bleed along the cream-colored paper in a strong structure.

"No. I have a son that is twenty and another daughter that is thirteen."

I exhale softly, releasing some of my disappointment.

"Are you married?"

The writing appears faster than I had first expected.

She blurts out sharply, "No, are you?"

I cannot help but to release a loud laugh to myself.

"No. No, I am not."

I fear that the dead end of the conversation will cause her to leave. I quickly scan my mind looking for something—anything to make her stay as long as I can. I find my response to her to be strange at the least, the new craving for another entity, shocks me slightly.

My fingers are unable to move at the pace of my desperation.

"Am I stealing too much of your time? Is it late where you are?"

My eyes look for the ink to bleed into view. Fear burns the back of my throat as nothing new has appeared yet. To my relief, I see the imprint of black ink bleeding along the pores of the page.

She swishes the form of her puckered lips to the right, "It is eleven o'clock at night here. What time is it by you? No, you are fine. I can stay up a little bit longer with you."

A slight breath of relief leaves my lungs.

"It is eleven here as well. That is cool that we are on the same time frame. I do not know how that is possible, but hey, I'll play along. Are you at home? Do you have to work tomorrow?"

I extend my left hand towards the bottle of vodka, that is calling out to me. I take a long drink as if I have been lost at sea for months and finally found land. I immediately feel the effects of the poison overtaking my blood stream to the point that I am no longer able to keep my eyes open.

I feel the weight of my head collapse into the center of the book. The outer casing of my vision begins to grow hazier by the moment.

CHAPTER THREE:

I hear the blare of my cell phone ringing through my mind. My eyes pop open in response. I lift my head gently from the page, extending my right hand towards the vibrations of the device. The name of a male rolls across the screen.

I groan slightly as my index finger knocks against the answer key.

My voice leaves my throat in a raspy sway, "Hello?"

The powerful shake of an uplifted tone blares through my pounding head.

I wince sharply trying to detect the letters from the maze of my current thoughts, "Hey! Do you have anything to send me for the new book, yet?"

I feel the weight of my head fall to the right, "No, but I think I have a great idea—"

The electricity in his tone chops mine in half, "Great! When are you going to send me the outline?"

I release a harsh groan, "Actually, I think this is something I want to wait until it is finished before I show you."

My heart begins to pound rapidly against my chest as I feel the heavy silence in the air grow thicker with each passing moment.

He quickly picks up his end of the conversation, speaking in a harsh phrase, "Okay. You know the rules, this isn't how we do things at MVC Publishing and you know that."

A slight pause forms into irritation as if he is attempting to readjust his words before I have a chance to react, "I think that I have been more than fair with you. I am not trying to put pressure on you here or anything, but things like this cannot be happening."

The structure of my body slides into an uncomfortable placement as agony scratches my throat, "Alex, I do not want you to worry. This book is going to be so amazing, you have never heard of anything like this. I promise, you will be happy with the final outcome."

My focus begins to drift from the current conversation with Alex, back onto the book.

My mind melts into nothing, but thoughts of my new love interest, Victoria.

The energy rising in my form from her dancing through my mind causes me to become restless.

I pull my figure into a full stance, pacing the room as I attempt to calm my racing nerves.

The thoughts of her can no longer be held in the safe haven of my mind, I find them leaking out of my mouth in a heavenly sway, "This girl, Alex. I just—I just wish I could explain to you how amazing she is."

I can almost see his eyebrows curve in confusion, "What girl? Sam, what are you talking about?"

His voice becomes drowned out inside of my mind as my main focus is shifted onto my words that are now hanging in the air in front of my form.

I feel the lining of my breath catch inside of my throat.

I lower the phone from my ear, pushing my body into an unstable walk.

My bottom lip drapes down with the emotions that I am currently unable to express.

The pixels of my vision jolt around my sockets, scanning the scraps of cream-colored paper that are now floating in mid-air as they exit my mouth.

I allow my mind a moment to process each item, they read:

"This girl, Alex! I just-I just wish I could explain to you how amazing she is!"

My shaken, right hand extends away from my form towards the shards of dead tree. The index finger and thumb of my extremity gently grasp along the paper that reads:

Is!

I feel the air snag inside of my throat as an unknown wind blows through the room from the left.

I attempt to release a scream of panic, but it would seem as though my vocal cords have been sealed shut.

Now, finding myself being unable to do anything, but watch in complete awe as the wind carries the pieces of paper towards the open book on the table. The clippings dive in a downwards motion, embedding themselves in the bulk of pages, disappearing from my sight.

I rush to the table, feeling as though I am unable to move my feet fast enough. I peer down into the leather binding to see that the words have been melted into the page, alongside the others that were previously written the night prior. My attention starts to pull towards the last fragment that lays in my hand. I can feel its energy wanting to advance towards the book as well.

Before I have a chance to fully understand what is going on, I notice that my body is slowly, piece by piece beginning to transform into the same material that I always am writing upon. The next thing I know, the weight of my left hand goes limp causing the phone to sail towards the floor, it rattles to a stern halt.

It is shot back to life by Alex yelling, "Sam? Hey, what happened?"

CHAPTER FOUR:

I feel the firm placement of my soles connecting to the ground. My pores begin to release a cold sweat as anxiety rolls through my blood, startling my body.

My vision feels like it is starting to fade, knocking me into a world of shock. I need to get some form of bearings, providing me information of where I am or what is going to happen. If not, I fear that I might lose complete control.

The sound of my own voice barging through my mind is beginning to be shut out by the soft, muffled tone of unknown voices coming from my right. They are surrounded by the delicate melody of a jazz tune soaring through the currents.

I turn my attention towards the vibrations, finding that they are coming from just on the other side of a thick, dark stained, wooden door that separates us. With my mind attempting to grasp reality, I realize that I am currently trapped in a bathroom.

The small, cube shaped tiles that reside under my feet are a dirty, off-white in color. I feel my body continuing to survey the rest of the area. I find that a rectangular, glass structure is hanging on the wall just above the tiny, yet bulky sink that is now showing my reflection.

I scan my form in a fast sweep, not seeing any visible injuries or faults causing me to relax immensely. I tilt my head to the right, admiring my attire of a black, button-down shirt, with the top, two buttons left undone and the bottom seam is tucked firmly into the waist band of my matching dress pants. The base of the legs rest just above my ankle allowing a full view of the shiny tint that engulfs my feet.

I take a deep breath, inching my body closer towards the ceramic, miniature tub. My right hand gently pushes the knob back allowing the valve to release a stream of cold water to rush against the cuffed bowl of my palms. I waste no time, splashing the beads of refreshment along my facial structure.

I swallow roughly attempting to down my fear as my shaken form strides towards the door. My unknowing, right hand extends towards the silver knob that reminds me of a twisted L symbol. The cool graze of the metal brings a flush of relief to melt over my heated palm. The weight of the door causes strain in the muscles lining the upper formation of my bicep. The crack in the door causes me to become bombarded by a mixture of over whelming sensations.

My eyes dart in a quick, side to side manner, revealing that I have suddenly found myself in an unknown environment, packed with strangers.

I can feel the rapid pound of my heart colliding against my chest as I attempt to find something to ground my mind.

To my left, is a large fireplace with a stone mantel surrounding the perimeter. The light brown, rocky surface sits nicely against the cream walls of the tight enclosure. Wooden tables of many different shapes and sizes line the dark hues of the wooden floor that creaks under my weight with every slow step forward.

My focus becomes shattered by the high-pitched scream of a woman's tone, "Sam!"

I can feel the weight of my form instinctively turn in the direction of the voice. I immediately notice the uplifting aroma of caramel, swirling together with the sweetened, bitter taste of a foreign coffee brew.

I am greeted by a rather small woman, she looks to be no older than eighteen but honestly, even with that fair judgement, I feel like my guess is really pushing the truth.

I scan her body with a fast motion, finding that her tan colored jeans are holding the bottom of her button down, long sleeve, white shirt between the band of her slacks. The cotton fabric of her attire is draped in the stiffened feel of a light green apron, tied around her mid-section in a messy bow.

Her right hand is extended in an unsure movement away from her form. Her knuckles are white, from the tight hold she has held along the cream-colored cup, crafted from cardboard. The exploding green hue to her eyes grows darker as uncertainty wraps her form. The lining of her cheeks brush with a light red, partially being hidden under lose strands of her dark brown hair.

Her tongue trips along the structure of her lips, "Here. I thought you might want this. It is really cold outside, you know."

I can feel the weight of my vision sweep between the black, plastic lid of the mug leaking steam and her.

My silence causes her to attempt to understand the confusion, "It is free. I bought it for you. It is on the house."

I feel the small tug of a smirk running along the right side of my mouth, "You really didn't have to do this."

She pushes the cup further in my direction, "We know."

I raise the drink towards my parted lips allowing only a small patch of molecules to rush over my tongue.

My eyes widen sharply as I evaluate the taste, "This is my favorite coffee. How did you know that?"

She shrugs her shoulders slightly in a sarcastic sway, "Oh, I don't know. You only come in here every day."

The shock in my voice overpowers her joking persona, "I do?"

Her reply is suddenly shifted in a different direction as her eyes dart towards the line of windows that cover up the front wall of the shop.

A gasp of anticipation flows over her words, "Oh, it looks like the owner is outside by your tent. You better get out there."

I can feel the light pressure of her fingertips pressing against the center of my back as she guides me to the exit which is constructed of two, matching, glass panel doors. She holds the one to the right of me open giving me one, last shove out into the rest of this world with her left hand.

I notice that the weight of my head pulls into a firm shake, 'I flinched under her touch. I do not even want to be touched by someone that isn't Victoria. How can I be so in love with a woman I do not even know yet?'

A small pause forms in my mind, 'I wonder how she is doing?'

I nearly trip as I stumble over the threshold, due to my distracted thoughts. The pounding rhythm of my feet trying to regain their structure along the wet concrete captures the owner's attention.

He turns towards me without hesitation. The tan tint to his flesh is partiality covered in a baggy, black suit. The small fragments of a white, button-down shirt underneath peeks around his neck. The glasses that are perched along the bridge of his nose, sets him into the age range of mid to late forties.

The energy that surrounds his form is drenching me in disappointment, "I am so sorry that tonight did not go as you planned."

He sighs deeply, "Well as either one of us had planned, to be honest."

His shoulders slouch, pushing his hands further into the deep pockets of his slacks.

I find myself beginning to scan my mind in search of an answer to this situation.

My vision melts to the scene that is just above his right shoulder. It gives me the knowledge of a decorated table, littered with books, but they are not just any paper bindings, these belong to me. An open laptop is positioned on the top of the table as well, blaring the tone of my audio books. Loose balloons are scattered along the ground, gently being pushed in different directions by the soft hands of the wind.

I can feel the weight of my form moving forward, placing myself between him and the book signing.

He follows my movements, matching me for every single one.

I cross my arms firmly over my chest, pulling down a mask of disapproval, "Yeah, I know. They could always be better, couldn't they?"

He drops his gaze towards the reflection of the store lights. They are radiating off the buildings in the strip as they glare against the puddles. The light of the dying sun that never got to fully shine its light due to the overcast is still lingering overhead.

I push my tone into a higher gear, "But, it is alright. There is always next time."

The air surrounding us immediately grows heavy with silence. To my right, I hear the fast knock of heels pounding along the rough surface, hearing this pique my interest. Something about that sound, it has always captivated me. Knowing that whoever is inside of them carries a strong personality. One of which, I find extremely attractive.

My vision is suddenly engulfed by the fast blur of a woman. The movements of her hair being shoved backwards from her forwards momentum has me completely mesmerized.

My mind quickly reels with the unsettling warmth in my form that washes against me, 'Something about this woman, it feels—familiar.'

I quickly turn towards the man, "Do you know her?"

His interest comes to life, throwing his head in the direction of my right, index finger.

I notice the pause in his reply as his tone softens, "Ah, yes. That is Victoria. She owns the salon just down the way. Really a great woman."

His voice begins to fade along the currents of the air as silence rains down upon us. He finds himself lost in thought about their previous encounters.

The energy shifts as his eyebrows contour in a sharp, inwards movement, "Why do you ask?"

I force a laugh to crawl up the back of my throat, "Just curious. She looks important."

He nods his head once in approval, pushing the upper-half of his body forward, extending his right hand. I meet him halfway, the clammy flesh of his palm touching mine causes a chill to run down my spine.

His words break against the humid air, "Again, I apologize for tonight. I wish the circumstance would have been better. I hope we can work together soon. Have a safe trip home."

I push my lips into a forced smile, "Yeah. Of course, anytime."

CHAPTER FIVE:

I catch a fast bite of the cool air brushing against my form. I turn my attention towards the pile of items that I know belong to me. I am trying to make any form of sense about what I should do from here.

I sigh deeply allowing my shoulders to drop along with my enthusiasm.

My mind begins to wander, 'There is no way that was actually her. The girl I have been seeing in my dreams for as long as I can remember. She is actually here, in front of me.'

The weight of my mouth is pushed to the right side of my face, in a tight hold, 'Damn, how drunk did I get last night?'

The explosion of anxiety running against my chest, floors my thoughts, 'Wait. Maybe, this is nothing more than a dream. I mean really, Sam think about it. You were writing about her just before you passed out.'

A deep breath drains from my bottom lip, "Okay, now all I have to do is prove this is not real."

My right hand automatically slides into the front pocket of my pants as I retrieve the handheld, electronic device.

The structure of my thumb applies pressure on the unlock button to the right. The illumination of the slick, touch screen reads, 7:45 p.m. on October 19, 2018.

I feel my eyes shift in a fast, side to side manner as I scan my brain for a logical answer, 'Okay. This is not a dream. Time does not exist in the mind, only in reality.'

I take a deep breath attempting to regain the structure of my own illusions. I feel my body shift into autopilot, grabbing the boxes of books.

I instinctively begin walking them towards the parking lot in search of my car. It does not take me long before I spot the familiar structure of my two-thousand and three, pitch black sedan that is sitting just across the way.

I approach the vehicle in a slow stride, my mind reels with confusion and shock as I peer into the drivers side window. I see that some of my personal belongings are sprawled out along the interior.

I prop the box between the backdoor and my torso, using the tip of my left hand to flip the handle in a sharp upwards movement. I hear the loud crack of the door being released from the seal, it rings through the empty air that surrounds me. I squint my eyes gently tossing the items into the passenger seat. They wobble slightly before jarring to a sharp halt after colliding with the plastic casing on the door. My left palm slams the door shut before I head back towards the tent to gather more items.

I notice that as I am walking up to the right side of the patio area, the sound of the metal door to the coffee shop creaks across my senses.

I quicken my pace, rounding the corner to find that the woman I had earlier mistaken for Victoria, is currently heading towards me. Just like in all of my daydreams and now, here she is in whatever version of reality this is, doing the exact same thing.

My mins soars, 'Sam, this is your only chance, this might be the only one you get. Say something, now! Anything!'

I step forward with my right leg attempting to gather her attention, "Do you like to read?"

Her figure comes to a sharp halt, "I love to read, why?"

I swallow harshly, hoping to dislodge the dryness, 'Wow. I have never had someone's voice make me feel so peaceful.'

I find myself wanting to hear more, when I suddenly realize she is waiting on my reply.

I force a fake laugh out of my mouth as my mind panics, 'Great! Now, what do I do? I never thought I'd ever get this far!'

I begin guiding her towards the front of the tent, "I am a published Author. Let me tell you about my books. I mostly write Fantasy, right now. It is the best thing I have written to date.

It is about an alien who comes to earth, to lure six, college kids to a small, bed and breakfast in Milwaukee, WI. When they get to the destination, the alien places them into the tenth room. During the middle of the night they are brought into the lobby. From there, they have to go through every room in the hotel to get back to room ten and win his game. Every room is a completely different dimension they have to fight their way through. Each world has a theme and a moral. It was originally supposed to be a self-help book, but I wanted to reach as many people as possible, so I turned it into a Fantasy as well. The first world is a reverse of animals and humans, it talks about animal abuse. The second world is based around the three different mythologies, it refers to power and greed. The third world is about an Indian tribe, who is born with earth animal tattoos on their chest. This allows them to bring out their spirit animals, it teaches spirituality and how to treat the Earth properly. The fourth one is about a paranormal house, the lesson is narcissism."

My thoughts are momentarily broken as I watch Victoria step closer to the book I was just speaking of. She runs the tips of her fingers along her lips in a thinking manner.

I smile gently, "The fifth one is about space, it informs you about how knowledge is power. The sixth one is a carnival theme that talks about mental illness. I wanted this series to reach all ages, from eight to eighty-six. No matter where you come from or who you are, you can connect in some way to this series. It is a great story, I think that you would really enjoy it."

I admire her silence as she appears lost in thought about something, but I cannot tell what it is.

She glides against the concrete in a confident stride, closing in the space that lays between her and the display set up in the center of the tent that is currently holding the bindings of my novels.

Her right hand grazes over the covers, her delicate touch makes me wish she would exchange the same form of affection with me.

I scan her figure in a fast motion, 'I always had a knack for tuning into people, being able to better understand them, but for some reason she is harder to read. Something about her is intriguing, yet something leaves me confused. I find it amusing that her exterior does not quite match her inner version.'

My thoughts are broken by her voice, "I want one of each. I will give them to my daughter. I think they could help her. I really wish you could talk to her. Maybe, it would be good for her. She is going through some really tough, personal things right now."

I nod my head once in understanding, "Of course, I would love to try and help. Just let me know when."

A smile breaks across her lips, "I will. Thank you again, for the books."

She extends her right hand towards me, I meet her halfway, feeling the warmth of her touch engulfs me with emotions that can no longer be contained. They boil over into my cheeks from the contact. I feel the release of her grip, the tingling sensation of her fingertips gliding along my palm, instinctively cause mine to close, hoping that I could convince her to stay longer. Only, her movements are too quick, I end up holding nothing more than the phantom weight of her absence. The next thing I know, she is walking away, vanishing from my sight.

A sharp shot of panic floods my chest, 'Holy shit. What do I do? Do I run after her?'

I feel the anxiety lingering in my form, no longer being contained.

My right foot begins to tap along the ground, 'No. Stop it. You need to calm down. That must not have been her. If it really was the woman of your dreams, it would have happened differently. She would have stayed to get your number, right?'

CHAPTER SIX:

I exhale my frustration trying to distract my mind, by continuing the cleanup process. I am so focused on the task at hand, I do not hear the approach of a person coming up from behind me.

The sound of their voice seems urgent, "Hello? It is me, again. I just wanted to come back by to give you this."

Her right hand is extended towards me. I try to hide my excitement of her presence, turning my attention towards the rectangle card she has in her hold.

She can sense the confusion dripping from my form, like a strong fragrance, "These are coupons for my salon. Just in case you want to come by for a haircut."

I am now unable to withhold my growing smile, "Wow. Thank you very much. I really appreciate this."

She confirms the acceptance of my gratitude with a slight nod, "I host an organization. It is a non-profit. I would really like to have you there. It would be great."

Before I have a chance to show my interest, I hear the relaxing vibrations of her words break through the air once more, "Here, give me your phone number. I will call you, so you can have mine. I'd like to talk to you more about the event I am hosting in a couple of weeks."

I waste no time in translating the information, "940-366-3454. I can't wait to hear from you."

The sudden shock of vibration trailing down my right leg, informs me of an incoming call.

I smirk, "Thanks, got it."

She pushes the weight of her figure along the structure of her left leg, "Good. We will talk soon."

I watch her walk away for the second time, it is revealing itself to be even harder than the last.

I whisper under the hum of my breath, "It will not be soon, enough."

The craving I have for her presence frightens me slightly as a thought sails through the chambers of my deepest memories, 'She is going to break my heart, isn't she?'

CHAPTER SEVEN:

With the last few boxes now placed in the car, I slide into the drivers seat, flipping the ignition on.

The vibrations of the vehicle coming to life rattle my thoughts as I move the gear into drive, pulling away from the shop, 'Wow, I cannot believe that I am actually here, in the same world as her. This is the best thing that has ever happened to me. I really hope she calls soon. I already am finding myself missing her voice.'

My mind freezes, jumping to another point of interest, 'This is so weird. I have never been like this before. I cannot believe the effect she has on me.'

The whimsical dance of my thoughts drives the car for me. It does not take long to travel down the vacant side streets towards my home. I leave all the items from the previous event in the car, feeling still slightly confused about my situation. I drag myself into the replication of the apartment.

Relief rushes over me as I find a spot to sit on the tan colored couch that is pressed up against the back wall of my living room.

The weight of my figure nearly collapses into a sitting position allowing my vision to become glued to the blank television, 'This is so weird. It feels like I am still on Earth, yet something about wherever this is feels different, but I am not sure why.'

I attempt to re-gain control over my emotions by laying down, hoping that in the morning hours of the next day, I will receive some clarity.

I extend my left hand in a downwards motion, retrieving the cellular from the hold of fabric. The swift motion of my thumb grants me access to the home screen. I release a strong breath of air, finding that I have yet to receive a text from Victoria.

While I am checking over my messages, I find myself constructing one of my own to Alex.

Hey, it is Sam. Could you give me a call when you see this?

Thanks.

I immediately notice the small, blue, spinning wheel sitting beside the words, informing me that it is incapable of being sent at this time.

A rough breath of irritation leaves my lips as I turn over trying to get some rest.

CHAPTER EIGHT:

I feel the gentle kiss of the sun's rays shinning in through my dangling, patio blinds. They shimmer along the structure of my face, pulling me into the world which I now know as my life.

I groan slightly, pushing my form into an upright, sitting placement. Immediately, my mind jumps to my phone.

I scroll through the notifications, feeling the weight of disappointment from not yet hearing anything from her.

My sadness shifts quickly to concern, finding that my urgent note to Alex was not received. I find this to be strange, seeing that I have four, strong bars of service in my upper, right hand portion of the screen. Part of me wants to go explore trying to defer the strings of this reality and to find Alex, hoping he could give me any advice on what is happening. Although, on the other hand, I find myself frightened of what could be lurking in the unknown.

I look around the area attempting to find something—anything to distract my mind from things while I wait to get in touch with Victoria. Ever since we have met in person, I feel like my mind cannot go a single second without going back to her.

Hours turn into days as I catch up on weeks of piled up work that has been growing around me for as long as I can remember. Finally, getting myself readjusted with work, I hear the ping of a text shooting through the stale air that surrounds me.

I feel as though I am unable to move quickly enough. My eyes scan the screen, finding a lengthy text appear from an unsaved number.

Hi, Sam. This is Victoria. We met the other night. How are you doing? I was wondering if we could set up a time to meet?

The muscles in my face appear to be stuck in a smiling placement.

Of course. I would love to meet up. How about
tomorrow, we could talk over coffee?

Her response is quicker than I anticipated.

Tomorrow sounds great. Where?

*I find my mind retracing a map of the local area in a fast sweep,
hoping that everything here in this dimension has in fact remained the
same.*

How about the one-off Park Vista?

*I do not close the app, finding myself re-reading the previous
messages from her in my head, not wanting to let go of this moment.*

Suddenly, a new one appears.

Sounds great. See you around 12ish?

The excitement building in my form causes my fingers to shake.

I cannot wait.

*Minutes turn into hours as she does not return a reply or initiate
any other form of a conversation.*

*My mind suddenly trails towards Alex, now that I know my
messages are being received causes worry to engulf my throat.*

*I quickly dial his cell, the fast blur of a dial rings through my
mind before the click of unachievable service pops in my ear.*

*I drop the phone from the structure of my face, 'I really hope that
he is okay. This is so weird.'*

CHAPTER NINE:

The next morning, I am awoken to the sonic boom of my phone's alarm bouncing off my empty walls. It causes me to shoot my body into a sitting placement, quickly tumbling with the device to shut off the sound waves.

I feel the stiffness growing along the structure of my shoulders, from the anxiety that is now haunting my dreams about the meeting later today. I cannot remember the last time I was this uptight about meeting a woman.

It would seem that my morning routine is taking much longer than normal as I am unhappy with all the attire I am trying on. It takes me a grand amount of time before I finally settle on the simple style of black dress shoes, a matching pair of pants with a dark gray, button down, long sleeve shirt. I glance into the mirror in my bathroom unsatisfied yet with the appearance, but at least I am ready.

I peer down at the tick of a clock strapped to my wrist, 'Just in time.'

I pump my body with a falsified courage, quickly downing a double shot of vodka before I exit the dwelling.

The radio crackles through one ear then out the other as I half listen to the anchor talk about the traffic conditions. My main focus remains on the upcoming engagement. I get to the destination early, hoping to beat her there. I quicken my stride once out of the car as I advance towards the front door.

I have to use all of my strength to pry the steel, glass panel away from the frame. I am flooded with the aroma of the freshly brewed coffee.

An older man behind the counter greets me with an unsure glance. The crooked, circular glasses that rest upon the base of his nose, cover the hazel tint to his vision. His black hair has streaks of gray, running through the maze of messy strands.

He speaks in a broken foreign accent, "How may I help you today?"

I scan the menu fast, perhaps too fast.

I do not pay attention to any of the words, I already know what I will be having, "A large, hot, caramel mocha, please."

He nods and proceeds to make the order himself.

I look around the small enclosure, seeing that a miniature post office is positioned in the back, right corner. The rest of the floor is cluttered with a variety of wooden table sets and large, redish, brown colored leather chairs. The kind that you would hope to see in a living area or office setting. I am unsure of where she would be most comfortable sitting.

I am still trying to make up my mind, with me being the only soul in sight, my options are limitless.

I hear the rough scratch of the man's voice, "Here, you go. One hot, caramel, mocha."

I flash him a fast smile, now feeling obligated to find a seat.

I feel the warmth of the beverage radiating through the paper covering causing my palm to leak sweat.

A table in the far back corner grabs at my attention. I slide into the chair on the left side giving me a full view of the entrance as I impatiently await her arrival.

It does not take long for the altering bell of the front door to ring through the humid air, informing the owners that another customer has entered.

My eyes melt over the figure of Victoria advancing in my direction. Her body is wrapped tightly in a light tan colored dress, designs wrapped in color form along the front structure, the length stretches to below her knees. Her arms are cluttered with bags and items that reflect necessitates of importance to her.

She sets down her belongings, placing them between the tabletop and the seat of her chair, "Hello. I am going to grab a coffee, I will be right back."

I smile while nodding once in understanding.

I cannot help but to watch her walk towards the counter. I find myself studying her every move, I find her walk to be sturdy and controlled, along the structure of the heels that are embracing her soles. She rests the palm of her hands along the counter, speaking in a quiet demeanor to the man, making it nearly impossible for me to make out her order.

I smirk to myself, tossing my attention towards the steaming cup of joe in my fingertips, hoping she does not catch my glare.

I hear the ping of her weight being carried forward, between the soles of her shoes, heading in my direction.

My head snaps forwards sharply, hearing the gritty grind of the wooden chair legs pull back, scraping along the dirty, tan tiles as she pulls it away from the table, only enough to allow her slim figure to melt into the structure.

I flash her a fast grin, only contouring the right side of my mouth, 'I wish you were mine.'

The gentle flow of my thoughts are broken by the shock I find in myself, 'Whoa, where did that come? I—'

The trail of my mind is shattered by her tone, "So, how are you?"

I raise my eyebrows slightly, 'A lot better now that you are here.'

I clear my throat quickly, altering the current path of my mind, "I am doing well, thank you. How about yourself? I just wanted to take a moment to express that I am extremely grateful, that you are taking the time out of your busy schedule to meet here with me."

Her shoulders push in a small, backwards movement, "Do not worry about it. I am sorry that I was late."

The weight of my head falls to the right, "It is more than alright. So, what would you like to talk about?"

Her vision drops from mine, towards the cup as she fiddles with the rim with her right, index finger, "I run a non-profit organization to help people. Everyone has a story that needs to be heard."

I nod my head in understanding, 'Ah. Okay, so you like to help people? I find this fact to be surprising.'

Before I have a fair shot to reply, she speaks again, "I want you to be there as one of my guest speakers."

A harsh laugh escapes my throat, "Why do you want me there?"

Her eyes line perfectly with mine, I can feel the chill of our connection running down my spine, "I think your story could help people."

I try to cover the sigh lingering over my lips.

She senses the shift in my tone attempting to ease my mind, "I will be interviewing you. Come on, it'll be fun. You should come."

My heart takes control of my vocal cords as I speak, "Yes. Okay, I'll go."

Her excitement of my decision enlightens me slightly.

The gentle nudge of a laugh knocks along the back of my teeth,
'I only wish that yes, wasn't for all of the wrong reasons.'

CHAPTER TEN:

Now that she has gained my approval of attending her function, I notice the tension draining from her shoulders as she talks to me about anything and everything.

Her voice wraps tightly around me, pulling me in deeper. I find myself more than ever, wanting to know everything about this woman.

While her words become planted along the structure of my brain, I find myself admiring her. My attraction to this woman is unlike anything I have ever felt before.

She moves her hands in an array of different directions as she shoots words all around me. I see the light in her eyes brighten as the conversation shifts towards her more personal passions.

My vision tilts onto the left wall, where the ticking hands of time knock against my mind.

A wave of silence engulfs us, her fading laughter lingers through the shop.

My voice burns against the stale air, "I am so sorry. I did not realize how much of your time I was taking up."

I catch her being unaware as well, glancing down to see the time.

Her eyes widen slightly in surprise, "Wow. It has been three hours. It did not feel like it at all."

A smile runs along the surface of my lips, 'Well, time sure doesn't exist when I am with you, does it?'

I yank myself back to reality, "It did not. I really have enjoyed talking with you."

She pulls herself into a full stance, following my movements. I find my body making its way around the right side of the table.

I am greeted by the warmth of her smile as her arms drape me into a warm hug. I press my body closely against hers. The rhythm of her heart escalates quickly. I am unable to tell who is more excited me or her? The weight of her arms laying along the structures of my shoulders is soothing. This moment is the first time I have felt at peace in ages.

I inhale deeply allowing the passages of my nose to be drenched in the strong hold of her perfume.

I feel her pull away, it takes everything I have inside of me to convince my hands to release her from my hold.

I try to hide my emotions, quickly darting to the door to hold it open for her. Then it would seem to me that I cannot move fast enough as I race to my car.

I feel the brush of wind from the left blowing against the sensitive flesh of my bare neck.

I find my body needing a fast moment to rest after just enduring the emotions I have never before felt in the coffee shop only moments ago.

I lean the structure of my form along the dusty surface of my vehicle. I hear the cheap panel of metal creak under my contact.

My shaken hands fumble in an attempt to remove the pack of cigarettes from the silk lining of my pocket.

Finally, I feel the release of the half empty pack resting in the sweaty grip of my left palm. I pick at the jagged, metal wheel on the lighter three times with my thumb, nearly rubbing the skin raw before I see a spark.

With the cooling effect of the bitter menthol now rolling a wave of relaxation through my soul, I find that my thoughts are beginning to wander onto Victoria.

Yet, to my own amusement, this acknowledgement does not surprise me. I knew the minute I saw her, she was going to be something special to me.

I begin picking through the files of my own mind, hoping to uncover answers for myself of what it is about this woman that has me so captivated.

CHAPTER ELEVEN:

I move my left arm in a downwards motion allowing my hand to follow its involuntary motions of knocking the extra ashes off of the stem.

The strong smell of her perfume gets shot into my face due to the wisps of her existence that still linger along the surface of my flesh. I have no control over my mind nor my emotions, feeling the aroma brings me back to the embrace. An uncontrollable smile grows against my now parted lips. A wave of warmth spreads like an intense explosion against the inner confines of my chest, making me wish that she was still wrapped tightly inside of my arms.

I feel the pressure of my phone in my left pocket urging for my attention. The next thing I know, I find myself panicking on the inside, almost like an addict, itching for my next fix as I type.

When do I get to see you next?

To my relief, her return is fast and sweet.

Soon.

I push a breath of air from my lungs, being unsure of how to speak to her. My thumbs brush against the letters in a slow manner.

Can I see you tomorrow?

I attempt to swallow, but my throat has become so dry it burns as I wait for a reply that is not showing.

I feel the harsh tint of anxiety rush over my brain, I try to calm my rigid form by hopping into the car and going for a drive. Sometimes, it is the only thing that is able to ease my mind.

I allow the surface of the new rubber soles of the vehicle to run against the pavement that creates the side roads which stretches out from the heart of the city like veins. With the max speed being a whole forty miles per hour, my thoughts dance along to some song I have never heard before on the radio.

The ping of an incoming text rattles my form. I reach for the electronic device that is carelessly perched along the structure on the wood colored, plastic console.

I divert my attention away from the broken, white lines of the lanes, towards my screen.

I see that I have been given a notification from my provider, stating that the messages I have so desperately been trying to send to Alex have failed.

The disappointment in my body is released along with my phone as it now rests in an upside-down manner in the passenger seat.

I know that I could drive from one side of the world to the other, but it still would not ease the friction in my soul as much as one moment with her.

I guide the axles of the vehicle to make a sharp, left turn pulling into the crowded parking lot of a strip mall near my house.

I park the car in front of a row of lights, shinning an orange tint against the top of my glossy hood.

It takes me only a matter of seconds to pull my form out of the cabin, being greeted by the cool, evening air that is blowing in from the north. I truck towards the double paneled glass doors, now carrying myself with a noticeable hop entangled inside of each step.

It does not take long for the booming vibrations of voices held inside of the confines to overtake the sound of my own, that was swirling around the idea of Victoria only moments before.

I pick my seat at the far, right end of the bar, making sure to leave as much space as possible between me and the other customers.

I find myself looking around in every direction. The rhythm of my right foot tapping along the surface of a wooden entity that is unknown to me, creates a song in my head that controls the fast pace of my paranoia.

I swallow hard, hoping that no one in the confined space has been made aware of my arrival, but it would seem that I am not so lucky. I can feel the heat of the drunken minds of dozens glaring against my figure.

The server's eyes ignite under the knowledge of my familiar presence.

His voice is strong, yet soothing, "Hey, Sam. What are we going to have tonight?"

I refrain from speaking as if to make it seem like I remain on the edge of multiple options that are floating around inside of my brain.

Do not be fooled, my mind has been made up since I left the coffee shop, "I think I'll do a double shot of my usual."

He immediately contours his entire face into a scrunched-up manner, "Those are absolutely horrible. I could never understand why you always drink that."

A slight grin melts against the right side of my mouth, "Only when I am looking for an escape."

His silence is broken by the sound of the glass colliding with the wooden surface of the counter, "Enjoy."

The molecules of the liquor make it to my stomach in record time.

I begin scanning through my messages, seeing that I had received one, seven minutes ago without my knowledge.

My heart begins to race against my chest, seeing that it is from Victoria.

Hello. How are you?

An invisible laugh attempts to escape the back of my throat.

I am well and you?

I extend my right hand to lay the device against the bar when the vibrations of an incoming message ring through my palm.

Good. I am sorry for the late reply. I got busy working. What are you doing?

The crashing blare of another drink being delivered to me snags my attention from our conservation. I inhale it quickly.

At the bar, on western center, having a drink. Want to join?

The structure of my right foot begins to pound against the metal bar positioned between the two, front legs as I try to remain optimistic about her possible response.

Yes. I will be there in ten minutes.

I feel the anxiety melt into excitement as I think about her presence. I find myself unable to remove my vision from the door, being far too focused on my thoughts, constantly reminding me that at any second, she is going to be right here, in front of me. The thought in itself is intoxicating. Suddenly, the blurred image of her figure engulfed by the rays of orange lights opening the door causes me to throw my vision ahead. I can only hope that she has not noticed me staring at her.

I attempt to readjust my now harsh breathing, but she makes it nearly impossible to even think straight.

Her footsteps are growing louder with each second.

The structure of her right hand crosses the corner of my vision, "Hello. Can I sit?"

I gently grasp her hand in mine, praying she does not feel me melt under her touch.

I nod my head once, the structure of my voice crumbles as it leaves my lips, "Yes, please."

I watch her delicately balance her weight into a comfortable, sitting position.

She side glances at the small sip of dark droplets that rest along the bottom of my drink, "What is that?"

My reply is held tightly by a laugh, "I doubt you would like it, not many people do. What do you want to drink? A vodka water?"

Her head nods slightly in agreement, her attention shoots without warning in an upwards movement as the man behind the counter seems to have startled her, "Vodka water. Coming right up, ma'am."

I cannot help but to release a small smirk as she begins to tell me about her life. I hang on to every word that drips from the chamber of her lips, finding that her tone is one of the most soothing sounds I have ever had the pleasure of hearing.

The direction of my vision has been scanning the area in a fast motion, noticing every tiny detail that surrounds us. The people, the smells, the voices of children laughing in the background, but most importantly, I find myself studying her.

The main focus of my sight is now being directed towards her eyes, they pull me into a state of emotions I am not used to experiencing. In fact, I am having a hard time trying to remember if I have ever felt like this at all.

Her pupils squint sharply, "You are everywhere but here. Why, am I boring you?"

I feel the punch of her words, stinging my mind.

I cannot control my head from spinning, 'Bored? Sitting here with you? The thought in itself is enough to make me laugh.'

A strong shot of air is pushed out of my lungs. I drop my attention in a downwards angle towards the fake hardwood floor.

I can only hope it is enough to hide my shock, "No. You are not boring me at all. I am here. Trust me, there is nowhere else I would rather be."

The weight of her head falls to the right, "Really? I do not believe you."

I find the structure of my body shift uncomfortably in the creaking hold of the chair, "You were telling me that you have a very secretive life. That you enjoy your 'me' time. You normally date younger men and you are like me, you honestly think that drinking gives you courage. You do not have a favorite color and that the common person's work ethnic irritates you at the lowest. Almost as much as you just became now, when you thought that I was ignoring you."

The surprise in her eyes fades as she blinks twice, speaking in a slight whisper, "You notice me."

I am unable to tell is she making a statement or again questioning my authenticity, "How could I not?"

Her face burns it a light blush as she gently runs her fingertips down my thigh, "Will you walk me to my car?"

My mind is currently unable to process the words that she has just spoken, it is far too focused on the fact that she just touched me so naturally. The thought alone, sends a shiver of hope down my spine.

I quickly find the foundation under the sole of my shoes, "Are you ready to go?"

She smiles brightly at me through the dim atmosphere giving me a slight head nod.

The silent air that greets us outside carries a bit of a chill, she begins to jog towards her vehicle. I find myself trailing after her like a lost puppy.

The thought of me having such a strong desire to be near someone shocks me.

My traveling mind is disrupted by her soothing tone, "Thank you for spending time with me tonight. I had fun."

I am unable to control the growing smile that begins to form along my mouth, "Of course, it was my pleasure."

She finds herself getting lost in my eyes, a grin begins to burn against the surface of my lips, 'Do not worry, angel. I feel the same way.'

Her eyes widen sharply as an idea shoots through her mind, shattering my train of thought, "I wanted to give you this. It makes me think of you and I want you to have it."

I tilt my head to the right, watching intensely as she digs through the passenger side floorboards. Finally, her posture evens out.

She turns her body slightly towards me, handing me a tall, ceramic, sugar skull designed coffee mug.

I take the item from her grasp, admiring it in silence. The base color is white with one skull lady on each side. Colors of pink, yellow, green and black explode over the sides, bringing it to life in my hands.

A thought zooms through my mind, 'You have no idea how badly I want to kiss you, right now. No one has ever thought of me like this. I wish I could tell you, but I do not think you would feel the same.'

She breaks my concentration, "I really have to go, it was nice seeing you. I hope you think of me when you use that cup."

CHAPTER TWELVE:

With the night now winding to a close, I find myself sitting in an almost vacant bar. Victoria has left me about two hours prior.

I am losing control to the drops of liquor flooding my system.

My focus remains wrapped tightly around her. Even in this distorted section of reality, she is my only concern.

I feel my mind casting off into a dream like sphere, where I wish I was hers. I find my deepest thoughts dancing with the idea of holding her tightly in my arms as each day comes to a close. Where I am able to find a peaceful haven. I try to imagine waking up every morning in a universe that turns solely due to her existence.

The burning hint of a satisfied grin quickly melts from my face, 'Come on. What am I even thinking? There is no way that she will ever look at me the same. Note to self: Do not get attached.'

I find myself glancing down towards my screen hoping that in this moment, she is somewhere thinking about me as well.

CHAPTER THIRTEEN:

Days have now passed with me doing nothing but work. I find myself clinging on to every moment I get to invest time into Victoria.

The days find us with conversations through the form of a text and the nights carry a different light.

I get to see her figure in front of me as we sit under a projection of stars and cheap drinks from the bar. The more about her that I learn, the deeper I feel my soul crave her.

I have contemplated expressing my feelings, but something always stops me. I am unsure what I fear more, her telling me that her emotions towards me are not the same or that they are.

I feel the urge to scream out in explanation of how I feel, it hits me the hardest when I see her completing the most trivial of tasks. These can include moving the straw around her glass, hiding from someone she knows who strolled into the parking lot or even something as simple as the wind gently blowing back against her facial structure as she stares off into the distance. She becomes lost in thoughts, that I can only find myself wishing I could be a part of.

I catch myself staring at her in depth, I cannot help but to wonder, 'Does she notice me?'

The next thing I know, our night is coming to an end, the way that most of them do.

The shorthand on the clock is just starting to stretch on past ten. Before she leaves completely, I feel the weight of her arms wrap me into a tight embrace. Giving me something to remember her by until we meet again. I watch her as she walks away with a sturdy stride leaving me as she goes to tend to her youngest child.

CHAPTER FOURTEEN:

I wake up, finding that my favorite day of the year has finally begun. My mind jumps into action, going a hundred miles an hour, 'October thirty first. Who could not love Halloween? I mean, it holds everything that is right in the world. Warm drinks, beautiful scenery no matter what direction you look, perfect weather and just a hint of superstition that you can smell in the air.

For me, normally Halloween means work. Thankfully, I have this bad habit of extending this one holiday out much further than the others. The whole month of October becomes a playground for me. The object of the game? Catch something real.

It is every author's dream, to find actual evidence of things that we spend our whole lives writing about, things that we think only exist in our darkest nightmares. Sounds great, right?'

I exhale sharply, looking around the empty walls of the apartment, 'Too bad I will not be doing that this year. I mean I could, but I do not think playing with a Ouija Board here is such a good idea. I do not even know what the hell is happening, yet.'

I find my gaze fixated out my patio window. The orange and yellow flakes of colors have shattered my mind, putting me into a far better mood.

The growing ring of my phone catches my interest.

It is my 6:45 p.m. alarm, informing me that I have to meet Victoria at a nearby bar and grill in fifteen minutes.

I made it out the door in what felt like a matter of seconds. This gave me more than enough time to sit in the parking lot and ponder our next encounter. The relaxing sounds of raindrops falling against the foggy windshield holds my attention.

A small vibration urging for my interest comes from Victoria, in the form of a text message.

Hey. I am inside. Where are you?

With my lost mind being pulled back to reality, I nearly jump out of the door to make it inside the building.

The pellets of water are breaking across my face, 'It's 7:21 p.m.'

A deep exhale of disapproval within myself is released as I see the time, 'She is early. This is new.'

Inside of the structure, I am more relieved than I would have imagined to be in a warm, dry environment. It does not take me long to spot Victoria to my left, sitting three tables back. The front of her body is revealed to the entrance.

I find the weight of my body being carried in her direction, "Happy Halloween."

She releases a fake laugh, "You too. Sit. Are you going to eat?"

The momentum of my body collapses into the dark red, thin cushion that lines the light stained booth.

I shake my head, "Not hungry, but I would enjoy a drink."

She looks at me from over the top of the plastic casing of the menu, "You need to eat."

Her tone is firm, but I am unable to tell if she cares or likes to have control. I find this thought to be rather intriguing either way.

I can feel the muscles lining my jaw tighten under the idea, "Okay, I will eat."

A sense of satisfaction from my approval of her demand rushes through her form. She uses just the tips of her fingers that line her left hand to nudge the other food directory towards me.

I scan the words in a fast sweep, already knowing what I am going to get.

The shadow from a young waitress in her early to mid-twenties is now intruding into our space. The enormous smile plastered against her glossy, red lips, adds to my irritation.

The weight of her dark, green eyes falls on Victoria, "What can I get you to drink, ma'am?"

It takes a moment of awkward silence to glide over the air before she breaks the tension, "Vodka and water and a plate of fries."

Her vision falls upon me sharply, "We will just share the fries."

The worker gently tosses her focus onto me waiting for my requested drink item, "Vodka and lemonade."

The thought of her demanding my next move causes stress to race through the right side of my jaw. I can feel the heat of the waitress staring at me as she awaits the movement of my approval.

The structure of my head falls forward before I throw my attention back onto Victoria.

The waitress nods once before disappearing out of our sight towards the kitchen.

I notice the focus of Victoria's sight is scanning me in a slow, vertical sweep, "Nice costume."

A ping of confusion springs through my mind. Suddenly, the realization of me being wrapped in a cheaply made plastic image of a firefighter's uniform melts across my memory.

A slight blush rolls along the surface of my cheeks, "Thanks. Where is yours?"

She pushes a long stream of air from her lungs, "I do not dress up for Halloween, but hey, you do you."

The small traces of sarcastic laughter get stuck in my throat, "That is too bad."

My mind begins to drift off to the last hours of the evening. When I was getting ready, I made sure to snap a more playful version of the costume. The portable memory card, portrays me, with the buttons of the top, left undone to show only my bare flesh underneath.

I relocate the image of time on my phone, slowly passing her the device hoping to get some insight to her feelings towards me.

I can feel the weight of my curious mind being held down against her. The structure of her shoulders tense slightly.

She attempts to hide her emotions by sliding the phone against the wooden surface in my direction, "Cute."

The night does not last as long as I would have hoped, but who am I kidding? Forever with her and I would still be itching for one more minute.

She has now left to go get some well needed rest. With me being well, me. I soon realized that after her departure, I could not waste a beautiful October night in my house. So, even with her absence, I find myself trying to make the most of the night.

On my way home, I find that the tips of my fingers are desperate for knowledge as I type.

So, I can tell that you like me.

Her reply is faster than I originally would have thought.

Yes. Was it that obvious?

    I smirk to myself, almost as if I am inside a realm of shock. I am unable to believe that here she is, the girl of my dreams and on top of it all, she likes me back. Before I am given a fair chance to respond, another one shoots in.

Do you like me, too?

    I can feel the stress melting from my back.

Yes. Yes, I do. You honestly could not tell?

    Again, no time is able to slip past before her comment is revealed.

No. I did not think that you would be interested in me.

    I feel as though my fingers are not going to move fast enough to properly gather my thoughts.

Why would I not like you?

    The light of my phone brings me more information.

I feel like this should be a conversation we have in person.

CHAPTER FIFTEEN:

Ah. The day I have been waiting for, her event. I could not decipher if my anticipation has been growing from excitement or fear. Either way, it is impossible to ignore that she has a strange effect on me.

I swallow hard, feeling the ball of my fear being pushed against the collar of my black polo shirt which is tightly knotted to the top button. I release my right hand from the wheel, wiping the clammy residue from my palm, onto the light gray slacks that cover my legs. The thin material that wraps my feet in a dark blue, argyle pattern is tucked away in the sturdy structure of my black oxfords.

I allow the robotic voice on the digital map, playing against the screen of my cellular device as it guides me towards Dallas.

I exhale roughly, in hopes of flushing out my discomfort with the situation. To my surprise, the directions are cut off by the vibrations of Victoria attempting to gather my attention.

I answer on the third ring, my mind is greeted by an uplifted tone, "Hi there. Where are you?"

I glance down at the time blinking in an orange neon number, informing me that I will get to the destination extremely early, "I am just now jumping onto 820. Where are you?"

I hear a breath of disappointment leave her throat, "I am here. No one is here, yet. Call me when you get closer and I will come down there to get you."

The disapproval in my current placement makes me chuckle, 'I guess, I am not early enough for Ms. Marquez. Why am I not surprised?'

The rest of the drive is quiet. I find myself attempting to sooth my anxious form by drifting away into the sound of the tires crackling against the pavement. It takes way less time than I thought it would to arrive. I park my vehicle into a public garage, just down the street from where her event is being held.

I do not even have a chance to turn off the engine when the zapping buzz of an incoming call drops my focus towards the console, 'Just the girl I was hoping for.'

I answer with a stale crack to my unused voice, "Yes, I am here. Just arrived. I had to park in the garage down the street."

An irritated sigh stretches through the currents, "Yeah, me too. The valet at the apartment complex made me move my car. I am pulling into a spot now."

The flash of headlights to my left, graze against my attention, a spot over, 'What a surprise. It is you.'

I attempt to shield my excitement from her, "I am next to you."

I push my thumb over the end button, without giving her a chance to respond. It takes me only a second to close the empty air that now lays heavily between us. She opens the weight of her door, nearly slamming it into me. Her body moves effortlessly as she slides out of the seat giving me a full view of her dark, fall attire. The base of her dark, stained jeans are tucked into her black boots that are decorated with small, fluffy pom-poms. A matching under shirt with a soft covering might be draped over her arms, but it melts into my mind.

Her hair bounces slightly as her loose curls attempt to settle, "Ready?"

Between the Pages

She closes the car door roughly, her face contours sharply almost as if she has forgotten something.

Using her right hand, she opens the vehicle one more time, her voice breaks in an echoing manner along the inside of the garage, "Oh! I was looking for this and here it is. It was on my wrist the whole time! I do not know where my brain is."

I do not say anything out loud, my mind is too busy admiring her, 'I really like the things about herself that she thinks are imperfections. To me, they are the best things about her. I only wish she could see herself through—'

The structure of my thoughts are shattered by her crackling voice, "Here, I want you to have this. It is very important to me, but so are you and that is why I want you to keep it."

My mind begins to swirl with confusion, watching her use her left hand to remove one of the bracelets from her wrist. She hands it to me in a gentle manner, I immediately show my appreciation by sliding it onto my wrist.

It is constructed from a bright red string, with a small bead in the center that reminds me of the all-seeing eye.

I flash her a fast smile, "Thank you so much. I really like this."

CHAPTER SIXTEEN:

Her energy always leaves me confused, I never know what she is thinking, but God I wish I did. There are times we are together I feel as though she might like me back. Then there are others, I feel like I might be reading into this wrong. I mean, she's literally, every single thing I ever wanted. I must have done something right, for life to reward me with her.

She guides me into an elevator allowing thoughts to flood the area around us.

I find my attention being peaked as she informs me of someone she invited, that she met online.

Her body language shifts, "It is not a dating site or anything."

I raise my eyebrows slightly, not understanding why she feels the need to explain herself to me.

A deep breath of irritation flies from my lips, "Okay."

I wish it did not happen, but I have to admit, hearing her talk about someone else, made me feel rather jealous. It put me in a bad mood the rest of the night. That is, until everyone else has already left and we now find ourselves waiting for two of her female companions to finish getting ready, so that we can all head down to a restaurant.

Now, with it being just me and her sitting alone in the lobby of her friend's apartment, I can once again inhale the feelings she carries for me.

My mind keeps trailing off to the events that occurred earlier in the night. The interview went pretty well, it was hard for me to take her serious when all I want to do is kiss her. Most of the event was in Spanish. I understand enough to get by, but when the conversations get heated that is when you will lose me. Victoria was great. She was able to see that I was having a hard time and acted as my translator.

The walk in the night air with these three women, makes me feel like I am on top of the world having Victoria strolling along the cement to my left. She looks to be a bit cold, holding her arms in a crossed manner along the surface of her chest.

In this moment, I wish that I would have been smart enough to think ahead into grabbing her a jacket, just in case she needs it. Hopefully, I will never make this mistake again.

I feel the bite of a nicotine fix running through my mind as I spot the green and orange lights of a gas station, yanking at my attention. The symbol of the store made me remember that I am out of cigarettes. We pass the store with a quick step, I do not want to bother anybody by asking if I could stop in for a second. So, I just stare at the glass doors allowing my mouth to water.

Anyway, it does not take long for something else to grab at my attention. With the lights at the corner intersection changing fast, the rest of the group is now ahead of me, pushing their weight back and forth between the soles of their shoes as they erupt into laughter about something I could not hear.

I see a flash of movement going in the direction of Victoria and the other two women. It does not take my mind long to process the image of two men, both wearing all black causing the tint of their light skin to appear brighter than it normally would. Their eyes hold a steady gaze forwards, but something about them it feels off. I find myself standing between them and her. I do not think that she even noticed that she was moments before being watched or that I was trying to protect her. Thankfully, this is a good thing for me. The last thing I want her to think is that I am already falling for her. At this point, the less she knows, the better.

CHAPTER SEVENTEEN:

We are all visibly thankful when we finally make it to the Mexican restaurant, getting out of the cold is a relief for us all. We are led towards the very back of the structure, where we find ourselves sitting in a large, half-circle booth.

Of course, I slide in on the outside, pressing the majority of my body against Victoria's. I feel her energy react in response to my gesture. The brush of her fingertips slide against the back of my hand from underneath the table. I try to hold my emotions inside, but I can feel the spark of a small smile boiling through my exterior.

This right here, is one of the many reasons why I find myself so captivated by her. She is a mystery, always leaving me wanting to know more. It is intriguing to know that she wanted to touch me as badly as I wanted to feel her warmth against me.

I want her to know that I wish she could do stuff like that more, but with the rules of our relationship, I do not want to push too far too fast. Losing what we are starting is not something I want to do. Not now, not ever.

I throw my head down in an attempt to regain my composure. The weight of the attention is shifted off of us and onto the waiter as he approaches me from the right side. He takes all our orders, gathering us each a drink and food. Me and Victoria decide that it is best if we just share a plate of food.

The food was great, but the conversation during the meal was awkward, I cannot help but to feel like they know more about me and her than they were originally letting be known. The thought in itself makes me uneasy. I do not want to stir up any trouble between her and her friends.

Thankfully, the guilt I am feel does not last long as the image of Victoria dancing to the background music brings a warm smile to my lips.

It does not take long for the waiter to see we are all finished and waiting on our checks. I find my right hand automatically reaching for the bill, when she swipes it out from underneath me.

She flashes me a soft smile, "I got this."

A small smirk rises to the left side of my face, I throw my facial structure in a downwards motion, hoping she does not notice, 'No one I've dated, has ever bought me dinner or given me a gift. This is a first and just one of the many reasons I want her.'

The brush of the fresh, night air rolling against my face brings me peace as we decide that it is best to just get a ride from a transportation application on the phone. It is too cold and the walk was further than anticipated on the way here.

Once the two are dropped off at the place of residency and another parking garage, me and Victoria find ourselves walking in a realm of silence towards our cars.

Now that we are out of the carpool lane and into the garage, the air begins to feel electric with our sharing of silent communication.

She smiles at me before disappearing into the darkness of the cabin that constructs the interior of her vehicle, "Follow me back home."

The racing pound of my heart becomes too much to contain as I practically throw myself into the drivers seat.

I feel a heavy weight of thoughts colliding into my brain, 'Wow. She really has an interesting effect on you.'

I shake my head gently, throwing the car into reverse, hoping to keep a hot trail on her. I feel excitement flooding through my body as

I follow the bright glowing haze of her taillights through the blurred image of the rest of the tipsy traffic littered along the roadway.

I inform her that I am in an urgent need to stop at the gas station to gather a pack of smokes. She guides me off of the highway towards the dim glow of a building in the middle of a creepy atmosphere.

It takes me three seconds to jump out of my car, entering into the crisp air.

I walk around the front of her car towards the entrance, it allows us to make eye contact as I pass. I try to hide the lingering smile that I cannot let go of, until I am already walking out the door with my items.

I stop by her window to give her a fast kiss before we head back onto the highway.

I begin to feel a heaviness fall against my eyes as the white lines begin to smear against my vision. My head pops up to attention as a patterned, vibration rings in my right pocket.

A calming sensation melts against my face as I answer with a relaxed tone, "Hello, beautiful."

Her voice matches mine, "Are you following me?"

I cannot help but to let out a small laugh, "No. I live five blocks from you. I do not think this counts as stalking."

A lighter glaze becomes draped around her words, "Do you want to see my house?"

I feel my head automatically nodding to myself as if she can really see me in the moment, "Yes. I would love to."

We stay on the phone as she begins to talk to me about her house, she takes me through a maze of darkened, suburban streets. I attempt to grab a form of bearings in the area, but my mind is far too distracted by her story.

A break in her throat causes my attention to refocus as the conversation is drifting in another direction, "Well, okay. Here it is. This is where I live."

I feel my foot remaining steady against the gas pedal, not wanting to be creepy as I pass her now parked car against the curb.

I am not able to see much other than the shadows of night casting over its figure.

My voice offers an explanation for my silence, "Thank you for showing me. From what I can see, it is very pretty."

I can almost hear her smile through the phone, "You are welcome and thank you for the compliment. I am going to go upstairs now and go to bed. You get home safe and we will talk tomorrow. Thank you for going with me to the event tonight. I had a good time."

All of the sudden, it seems that with the acknowledgement of our time together coming to an end, makes my mouth unable to move fast enough, "I hope you have a great night. Sleep well and thank you for inviting me. I had a really good time as well. Thank you for showing me your house. Sweet dreams, sweetheart."

I hear the motion of her thumb cutting off our line.

I find myself left in the silence that engulfs the cabin of the car. My mind should be focusing on the road, but instead my vision keeps swaying towards the stars. They make my mind wander towards Victoria, I become slightly frightened by the heaviness that lines my chest when she is not around. She makes missing her feel like part of me is absent as well.

CHAPTER EIGHTEEN:

The day started off as a typical one would. I drag my figure into a hazy mess from the couch to the kitchen. The reflection of my worn-out form is shot through my mind as I pass the microwave, on my way to start up the first pot of coffee.

My mind appears to have two things on it, but one screams much louder, the urge of a nicotine fix. I can feel the bare soles of my feet grinding against the strands of carpet with every step towards the patio door. With my legs feeling like they weigh a hundred pounds, my trip outside is taking much longer than usual. My mind becomes louder as I fumble with the lock.

Finally, I am able to step outside into the chilly atmosphere. I immediately feel the kiss of the breeze awaken my soul as I quickly light my cigarette. I re-enter the house with a now, clearer image of my surroundings and a slight hop in my step.

The smell that can be enjoyed lingering along the currents of air ignites along the structure of my brain with excitement. I love the aroma of menthol, swirling together with bitter coffee beans. I take one more deep breath allowing my lungs to have a real taste, guiding my weight towards the couch. I plan on spending some time meditating before fully starting my day.

I can feel the latches of my mind slowly beginning to unravel, when a loud ping interrupts my thoughts.

The blood shot surface of my eyes scan the surroundings. I find that it was my phone that has made the unsettling gesture. It was trying to inform me of an incoming message from Victoria and I am thankful that it did.

Good Morning, love.

Do you want to come over later? We can open that bottle of wine you gave me.

I feel the currents of my mind raking through memories when a strong smile, melts across my lips.

I can feel my gaze intensify as my thoughts hold me tighter, 'Ah, right. The bottle of red from California. It was intended to be saved for a special occasion. Only, I cannot seem to think of anything more special than you.'

My brain's tone is shattered by the motions of my thumbs as I type back.

I would love to. What time?

My mind begins to trail off with a thought, one of which I have never openly admitted to myself until this moment, 'I do not know why, but knowing that she wants to see me, she wants to spend time with me, it means more to me than she will ever know. I have never had someone care so much about me that they could see me every single day and not get bored. When I say that she is literally the woman of my dreams, it should not be taken lightly.'

I sense the muscles lining my shoulder blade shift as I attempt to place the phone down. Before I get the chance, another notification from Victoria swarms in.

6. See you soon.

My eyes glance in an upwards motion, calculating that I have close to four hours to prepare for this. I take a deep breath, forcing my head to stay on the right path, getting me out of the house before I even realized what has happened.

I feel the air catch along the tunnel of my throat as I park the car out in front of our meeting area. I convince myself to get out of the vehicle and into the brisk, night air. With nothing more than an empty strip mall to keep the area filled.

My body reacts to the enjoyable weather conditions as I inhale deeply. I allow the flavor of beginning dreams mixed with the faint taste of nature to coat my tongue.

The slight tug of a vibration coming from my front, right pants pocket catches my attention.

I feel the gentle slide of a smile running against my mouth when I see that it is, in fact who I was hoping it was from Victoria.

Come on through the back doors. The front is already locked for the night.

Unable to hold back my smirk any longer, I shove my phone back into the fabric holder as I make my way to the rear entrance. I feel the weight of the door nearly knock me over as I stubble backwards as it breaks itself free from the latch.

The soft light from inside the room blares against my figure, casting a similar shadow to my back.

My eyes sweep the area quickly, seeing nothing more than a fast blur of white. Finally, my vision collides against Victoria, who has now stood to greet me.

My eyes close upon impact of our bodies touching.

My mind begins to reel, 'You feel like home.'

The weight of my thoughts causes my vision to drop.

Her posture shifts to a confused concern, "Are you okay?"

I feel the false lining of my voice as it travels out of my mouth, "Yes. Of course."

Uncertainty floods her form, "Okay. If you are sure."

She pauses for a small breath giving me a moment to object the conversation. When no sound arises from my chest she continues.

Now, speaking in a smoother tone, "Here. Have a seat."

Her right, index finger guides my attention to a thin, metal, folding chair.

I allow my figure to adjust against the creaking surface trying to find a spot that is comfortable. I hear the buildup of air gently leaving the cushion on the peeling, black, leather cover of her office chair.

Her smile beams, even in the darker surroundings, "Are you ready to try the wine, now?"

I nod once, leaning forwards slightly. I allow my right, index finger to lay against my sealed lips. My voice would come out too high pitched from nervousness if I even attempted to relay any form of an actual answer.

I find myself trying to remain discreet while I admire her every motion. Her arms hold steady while she pours us both a half glass full of the ruby red wine that bubbles as it attempts to settle into the new container.

Her tone drifts off into the air that surrounds us as she begins to tell me about her thoughts, her hopes, her desires. The details that you have to work to know are the best.

I pull myself into a full stance trying to get to the bathroom. She follows my gesture, raising herself to my level.

She begins to close the gap of air between us with a quickened step. She gently pushes me against the wall as the rest of her body now lays tightly pressed against me. Our lips find themselves entangled with our first kiss.

My mind tries to hold me in the moment, but there are too many different emotions that my mind is trying to maintain. A small moan slips out of my throat as she kisses me deeper as if she has been craving me all of her life. I do not mind, the feeling is extremely mutual.

I feel her smile as she tries to pull away. Her eyes meet mine and I feel the overpowering urge to feel her against me one more time. I wrap my right arm around the small area of her waist pulling her closer. Feeling her chest brush against mine as we match each other for every breath, makes me feel like I am the luckiest person in the entire world to be here, sharing this moment with her.

The sound of her lips breaking away from mine causes my soul to want more, but the mood soon shifts.

She breaks my thoughts trying to catch her breath, "Ah. I love kissing you. I love feeling your body against me. I love touching you."

She pauses, shifting the tone of her voice to a harsher vibration, "Two things. First, I will never have sex with you. I will only make love to you and in order for that to happen, we have to be in love first. Second, let's get something clear right now. I will never need you. I may want you, but I will never need you."

I feel my weight making me take a small step back while nodding my head in understanding.

The shadows that fall against her eyes lighten as she gently kisses me one more time before allowing us the pleasure of eye contact, "Thank you for a great night. I had fun. Are you ready to go?"

With me now on the road heading back home, I get an incoming call that nearly startles me so badly I could have gone off the road.

I answer in a faint whisper, "Hello?"

The gentle sound of her voice trails through my brain, "Hi there. What are you doing?"

A slight laugh slips out of my throat, "I am driving home. What are you doing?"

She sighs softly, "I am doing the same thing."

I swallow loudly, "Are you okay?"

She nods as if I can really see her in the moment, "Yes, I am fine. I just miss you already and wanted to hear your voice. Will you talk to me until I get home?"

The words nearly get caught along the structure of my throat, "Yes, of course. I miss you, too."

Before I know what is happening, me and Victoria have already said our good nights. She is safely at home and now, so am I.

An incoming text makes my figure jump.

Good night. I cannot wait to see you again.

I feel more confused than ever, one minute she says that she does not need me then the next, she makes me feel like she needs me just as much as I need her, but I am always left unsure.

The thing she does not know, I wanted nothing more than to call her the minute I leave her side. No matter how much time I have with her, it never seems to be enough. It is comforting to know that she might feel the same way about me, but like she always tells me, only time will tell.

CHAPTER NINETEEN:

The next morning, I find myself awoken to a harsh jolt as my body frees itself from the dark hold of my nightmare. The deep gulps of breath have me stuck to the couch for the time being. My vision closes tightly as I play back the scenes of my dream,

The outer lining of the surroundings looks like nothing more than a black, hazy mist.

The only thing I can focus on clearly, is the replaying memory of my ex-girlfriend saying, "I will never need you. I might want you very bad, but don't you dare ever think that I would need you because I don't."

I use my right hand to viciously rub my face, hoping to erase the fragments from my mind.

The release of a large puff of air relaxes my chest. Now, that I feel calmer, the call for coffee and a cigarette are getting far too loud for me to ignore. Finally, the morning is starting to turn around.

I use my right hand to search for the remote, putting on the stock market, in order for me to stay updated all day with the sound set to mute.

The soft movement of my cellular device, skidding against the wooden surface of my dark stained coffee table steals my interest.

My eyes attempt to adjust to the falsified light as I read a new message from Victoria.

Good Morning. Thank you for the wine. I liked it. How did you sleep?

I smirk as I shake my head slightly.

Good morning, beautiful.

You're welcome, Anytime. It was good and yours?

I feel a surge of anxiety flood my body as It reacts to the sound of my mind, 'She will never truly love you. You heard her say it last night. Do not fool yourself into believing something different.'

I shake my head sharply, shattering my negative thoughts as I hop into the kitchen to get a cheese stick for a snack. I begin to open the clear, plastic wrapper to allow me access to the white hue of the cheese, when a loud ping radiates from my phone.

My pace quickens as I rush to the couch.

It was okay. Could have used some more sleep. I have to work a lot for the next few days. So, I will not be able to see you, but we will stay in contact.

It is hard to ignore the small tear of sadness, the thought of not seeing her brings me.

The realization of my own activity nearly brings me to my knees in utter shock, 'This isn't good. I found out yesterday that I will never be something serious with her. She assumed I wanted nothing, but sex and I assumed she wanted something more than a distraction. I guess maybe, we were both wrong. Either way, it does not set well with me. I feel like I am missing something here and I crave the deepest desire to know the truth.'

I release a raspy grunt of anger from my lips as I pull myself back onto reality trying to adjust my mind, 'It is okay. Relax, Sam. She is not your ex. She is different.'

A faint echo of a confirmation follows the next one, 'You are right. You are doing the right thing. Give her a chance.'

My delay in the conversation is seen by her as unusual. I normally waste no time to get her an answer, so she tries again.

What are you doing?

I internally smile at her obvious urge for my attention. I really enjoy the thought of her wanting me like this. It is good to know that she craves me as deeply as I do her. I just wish she would show it instead of keeping all of her feelings hidden that is, if she has any for me at all.

My thumbs act quickly, scrolling down a response.

I am glad you slept well. I am sorry to hear that you have so much work and yes, let's stay connected. I am still trying to convince myself to start the day. You?

My eyes burn slightly as I scan her letters.

Me too.

I smirk at the thought of her lying in bed in her casual state, rather than the professional one that I am now so accustomed to seeing.

My distracted mind nearly misses the silent alert of a new text.

Can we talk about something?

It is as if I can feel the intensity through the screen. This feeling drastically shifts my mood to match hers.

Yes. Is everything okay?

    I sit in a confused realm of anxiety. My right foot taps against the carpet as I try to alleviate some stress while I wait for her reply.

I know that we have been seeing each other for almost a month now. I know that no one knows we are together yet, but people cannot know about our relationship. Not right now. Just give me some time to get everything settled. When the time is right.

    I read this one with a heavy wind of sadness draining through the phone.

    I begin searching my mind looking for an answer, 'You can handle this. It is okay as long as me and her stay loyal to one another, we can make this work. She is worth it. You know she is.'

    The rush of positiveness, nudges me in the right direction of writing back a text.

That is okay. We can figure this out together.

    It does not take long for her to re-direct the conversation.

Talk to me, tell me about yourself.

    My mouth twitches slightly.

What do you want to know?

    The beat of my heart becomes amplified as I wait.

Surprise me.

    My mind releases a large breath of disorganization, not knowing where to start.

I love to play pool, motorcycles, history and art.

My thumb moves faster than my brain, forcing me to begin composing an ending text to the last.

I am not sure what else you would like to know about me, but it would be much more fun if we talk about you.

I gently place the phone down on the table. I attempt breaking my attachment to the device, that only seemed to develop when I met Victoria. My eyes continue dancing towards the darkness of the screen, hoping it will bring a piece of her closer to me.

I try to distract my mind by lighting a cigarette, forcing my lungs to slow down as if mentally giving myself a countdown to push my brain towards a different direction. Unfortunately, my attempt at buying her time, comes to be a bust, still nothing.

I deeply exhale, turning all of my attention towards work. It does not take long before I feel my mind slowly making its way back to her.

I throw all of my weight into the backrest of the couch, placing my face in the crevasse of my palms, 'No one has ever had this kind of effect on me. I am not sure what exactly this means, all I know is, what I have with her, I never want it to end.'

CHAPTER TWENTY:

My right sole taps gently against the light brown, tile floor. It dances to a melody that only exists in my own thoughts. I can feel the anxiety rising through my hunched over state as my eyes scan the area.

Currently, I am finding myself sitting in the corner, left side of the empty room of a sushi joint. It is located less than a block from my house. The only movement I have seen in the last fifteen minutes has been from the half-alive staff that keeps walking purposely past me. They nod their heads with sympathy filing their fake smiles.

I deeply exhale, looking around at the vacant, deep brown rows of chairs and tables that construct this portion of the eatery. To the right, is a liquor bar, next to the sushi counter. An elderly man is falling asleep as he awaits the twelve o'clock lunch rush that is happening in roughly thirty-four minutes.

My mind drifts back towards the time, wondering if she has forgotten about our date. I find myself walking towards the front doors at a fast pace. Relief only floods my mind when the cool breeze travels over my skin. I can feel the tension in my vision automatically pull into a contoured angle attempting to protect my pupils from the sun's rays.

The weight of my body gets pressed up against the shades of red minerals that create the brick wall. A familiar color and brand of car pulls into my view from the right.

I inhale a long drag from my freshly lit cigarette. Her eyes meet mine as she gets out of the vehicle and begins to walk in my direction.

Her flawless figure is wrapped tightly in fall attire, with the main hue of choice being black. She looks good, but even all the complimentary words in the English language would not be enough to truly grasp how beautiful she is.

She greets me with a bright smile, gently pulling me closer for a small embrace. The tingle of her breath, lining against my neck causes my weight to press tighter against her.

She releases a playful giggle in response, "Are you ready to go in?"

I pull my figure away from hers as I inhale one last drag from the half stick of my tobacco that still remains.

I toss it to the sidewalk as I promptly hold the door for Ms. Marquez to walk in first.

The waitress to greet us at the door scans me in a fast sweep, her voice travels through the air in a fast, unclear manner, "Just the two of you?"

Victoria nods once, only replying in a whisper, "Yes."

The woman takes off at a quickened pace, leading us towards the table by where I was seated earlier. Once we both sit, the waitress flashes me a nervous smile. She is attempting to get my approval of how she handled the situation.

A silent laugh is melting into the currents of my mind as I nod once.

She tries to hold back a smile, "Someone will be with you shortly."

Victoria did not seem to notice the mysterious behavior of the waitress. Thankfully, because I really did not know how I was going to explain what just happened.

Our sushi comes to the table, not long after ordering. It is demolished one bite at a time as we engulf ourselves in conversation. Time always seems to fly by when I am with her. It is quite a sad feeling; I can never seem to get enough of her.

We are now sitting in the drivers seat of her car. Yes, we are tightly squished together, but we both seem to like it.

I watch her attempting to re-adjust her position, "Me being friends with my exes. That does not bother you?"

My mind begins to shift through my thoughts, I shake my head in return to her question.

She glares into my eyes as if some secret can be seen through the window of my soul, "You'd be easy to cheat on."

My heart begins to feel like someone just injected me with panic, "Why do you say that?"

Her eyes reveal confusion with my response, "You are too trusting."

My body slouches slightly, shifting the entirety of my mood.

My mind explodes over the different sensations, 'Is she going to cheat on me? Is that her way of warning me? I mean, why would I accuse her of doing something like that? I always give trust until proven otherwise. It should not be something that is earned, it should be given. Now, due to that statement, it really got me thinking—should I be worried?'

CHAPTER TWENTY-ONE:

A few days have passed since my last encounter with Victoria in person. Three, sleepless nights, two bottles of vodka, fourteen pots of coffee and two cartons of cigarettes later is not enough to mask out the sound of her telling me that I am easy to cheat on as it roams around inside my mind.

I can feel my brain being overtaken by the fragments of a memory building inside of me. Back to all of my ex-girlfriends who cheated on me. The feeling of worthlessness begins to leak across my body.

I lay my head into my palms, hoping that using my inner hands to rub my closed eyes will wipe the thoughts from my sight, 'Maybe, Victoria is right. Maybe, I am easy to cheat on.'

My self-loathing is shattered by a ping on my phone, it is from Victoria.

Good Morning, love. We should have coffee today @12. Want to go to the one we met at?

It takes my brain a minute to clear out the grog, before typing my reply.

Good morning, beautiful. Yes, that sounds great! I cannot wait to see you!

She shoots back into my device.

(: Me either.

I find my legs feeling heavy from the lack of sleep and it looks like I forgot how to button my black dress shirt, 'Uh. I can't catch a break here lately. Now, she is going to think I am easy to cheat on, I am too nice and I look like hell.'

I feel an immediate shift in my energy as she appears in my line of vision.

My voice cracks through a smile, "Hi. How are you?"

She removes the tinted surface of her glasses, "I am good. Are you ready to get some coffee?"

I nod in agreement. I find myself rushing around her allowing me to get to the door first. I watch her glide along the threshold in a confident stride. She scans the area as if she is looking for something, but I am never sure what it is that she is watching out for. She slowly guides us through the familiar layout of the floor plan.

My mind carries me back to the first night I was allowed into this reality and how this whole dream like state started here.

My brain begins to focus on the menu, seeing that we are now getting closer to being able to order.

The same staff from the last time I was here is on board.

The excited woman that gave me free coffee a month ago is now standing on the other side of the counter, "Hi, Sam. What can I get you guys?"

I pass her back a soft grin, turning my main attention onto Victoria. I use my left hand in a polite motion, informing her to order hers first.

She steps forward, placing her soft palms against the gritty, dark gray countertop, "I'll have a small, non-fat latte."

The barista types in the order quickly before turning towards me, "And for you, Sam?"

I step forward with my right leg, "A medium, hot caramel mocha, please."

She smiles widely once the order is complete, reading out loud the total.

Me and Victoria both begin fighting over who is going to be the one to pay.

I laugh gently inside as the woman takes my money over hers.

I glance over at Victoria as I think, 'She is cute.'

I wait at the counter for the drinks to be finished while she finds us a place to sit. It does not take long before I find myself sitting down as well.

She takes a small sip of her coffee, fragments of her lipstick become stuck to the white rim of her plastic lid.

She uses her right thumb to clear the mouthpiece slightly, "This is hot."

My face scrunches slightly, "Be careful."

Her eyes dance up towards me, "Do you know what today is?"

I nod once in certainty, "Yes. It is November 19, 2018. A month since we first met."

She hides her face slightly behind her cup, "We should do this every month on the nineteenth, have coffee."

I agree with no thought of hesitation.

We become draped in shards of conversations.

My mind begins to travel with thoughts, 'I like that. It was the start of me and you. Happy one month, Victoria.'

CHAPTER TWENTY-TWO:

With the Thanksgiving holiday now slowly creeping past us, things start to drift back to normal. My phone begins going off at 11:57 a.m. The static anxiety flooding my body begins to lessen when I see it is Victoria.

I answer with a crackling tone, "Hello?"

My ears are bombarded by the sweet canopy of her voice, "Hi there. How are you?"

I smile to myself, "I am well and you?"

A pause in her thought stalls the conclusion of the conversation, "I am good. Thank you. I was wondering what you were doing today?"

I can feel my heart beginning to pick up speed, "Just working. Why? What's up?"

Her tone gleams slightly, "Me too. Do you want to come up to the salon and we can work together?"

My mind begins to sail off towards my work pile, but it is the farthest thing from my priority right now, "Yes, I would love to. When?"

Urgency runs through the static currents, "Right now."

I nod my head once in understanding, "Sounds great. See you soon."

Before I am able to say anything else, she closes the line, "Bye."

My lips crack trying to release the word, "Bye."

The faded response of her saying, bye one last time echoes through my head as the dial goes dead.

I exhale gently, moving my body in a rush. I quickly toss on a black pea coat, grab my work bag from off of the floor and stumble out into the frigid air.

The darkened clouds that shade the air hold a spooky atmosphere that now surrounds me. I inhale a deep breath of the refreshing scenery. I love days like this, they leave the world in a hint of mystery.

It does not take me long to arrive at my destination. There are not a whole lot of bodies out on the roadways. I imagine they are either curled up at home under a blanket by the fireplace with a good book or they are still trying to recover from the food coma, thanks to Thanksgiving.

Regardless, I am happy about getting to see her sooner than I originally assumed.

I walk into the back of the salon, where I was previously directed moments ago by an unopened text from Victoria.

I carry myself through the entrance, getting hit by a bright, white light.

It shines greater than the last time I was in this room. While my eyes are attempting to adjust, my ears become flooded with the sound of women laughing in the front.

My attention reconstructs just in time to get a perfect view of Victoria, who is now standing to greet me. Her feet are wrapped tightly with a black boot with small, fluffy spheres dangling from the laces. The smoothness of her legs are covered in a floral designed stitch, residing under the stiffness of a tan skirt. The seams of them ride up to her mid-thigh with every step towards me. Her arms extend towards my neck causing the sleeves of her black dress shirt to pull by her shoulders, I notice that the bottom of the shirt is being secured in the waist band of the skirt.

The brush of her skin against mine, sends a shiver down my spine. The intake of air from my last breath gets caught in my throat, making it impossible to speak. She gestures for me to have a seat, I follow her silent commands as instructed. My eyes hold a steady gaze against her as she finds her seat and begins working.

She side-glances at me, "What are you staring at?"

My cheeks burn red under the acknowledgement, "You."

Her attention shifts back to the screen, "Why?"

My mouth twitches slightly, turning to hide a smile, "You are beautiful. I cannot help it."

Her focus remains on the false light of information as her left hand extends towards me, resting along my thigh, "Work."

A slight smirk runs along her mouth.

I finally find enough strength to attempt to pull my actual focus onto work. It does not take long for the silence between us to become broken by the sound of a door opening. I am unable to see who it is, due to my back being towards the entrance.

I am able to tell however, that the person approaching is just one of Victoria's hairstylists by the tone of her voice shifting, "Is everything okay?"

The woman stumbles over her tongue, "Yes. Sorry, I did not realize you had someone in here. I'll come back later."

Victoria motions her hand in a relaxed, carefree gesture, "No. It is okay. This is my friend, Sam."

A slight pause forms as we make eye contact, "My best friend."

My vision drops towards the ground trying to hide the truth from the rest of the room.

The air is broken by the woman, fading from the room as she turns to leave, "Thank you, but I will just talk to you later."

Victoria smiles at me speaking in a soft whisper, "They are talking, you know."

My vision squishes together, "Who?"

She throws her head towards the other room, "The girls."

This only leaves me with more questions, "What are they talking about?"

Her eyes appear to be filled with shock, "Us. They see you here all the time. You bring me gifts and we were jumpy when they walk in."

She pauses slightly, using her palms to run along my thighs in an upwards manner, giving me a long kiss, "They are going to think something is going on between us."

The weight of my eyebrows rises slightly, "Good. Let them."

She smiles, shaking her head slightly, moving her attention back onto work, "I do not care if they know. I am mostly concerned about my parents and my kids finding out."

My heart begins to pound faster at this information. I throw my facial structure towards the floor, hoping to hide my smile. I know I am not supposed to, but I cannot help it. All I can do is get lost in her. The way she walks, talks, kisses, touches me. It completely consumes me. In a way, I never before knew was possible. My mind begins to twist slightly, 'I am in love with you.'

CHAPTER TWENTY-THREE:

A few days have now passed since I last saw her.

My mind is not allowing me to think about anything other than the fact that I am in love.

My acknowledgment only makes it worse, 'I want to tell her. Maybe, she will tell me first. I do not want to tell her then her not feel the same way about me, but I also do not want to make the mistake of keeping this information to myself.'

My mind takes a moment to allow the last thoughts to fully sink in before another begins, 'Here I am, madly in love with a woman, who might not stay. I do not want to tell her and ruin what we have or freak her out, but at the same time, tomorrow is not promised. I am scared that I might not ever get another chance. I know that she hates when I think like this, but the reality of it is far too real.'

I inhale sharply, hoping to resort my brain, when an incoming notification shatters my interest, 'I hope it is Victoria.'

It takes my mind a second to re-read our previous messages. I sent her one a few hours back, asking her if she was having a good day.

My thoughts remain unsure as my thumbs shake.

Good. Hey, I have a weird question.

If you fell in love with me, would you tell me?

She opens the message immediately, part of me wants to wait to see what she says, but the other part does not want to look desperate. I lock my phone. It unlatches itself, informing me that she has replied.

It takes me a moment to grow my nerves to open it.

I will never fall in love with you.

I exhale deeply, it feels like every bone in my figure has just been shattered into a million pieces. Before I have time to gather an answer. I see through blurred vision, that another message has just come through.

I would wake up in love with you, but yes, I would tell you.

My mind floors with emotions, before I am able to completely calm down, I type my response.

I am in love with you.

The reply is nearly instant.

You are?

I gulp as anxiety floods my form.

Yes. Is that okay?

My breathing becomes shallow and short as I try to ensure I do not miss the notification.

Yes. I am in love with you, too.

I am unable to hold in any kind of internal happiness.

My mouth explodes into a gigantic smile.

You are? Since when?

Her reply is taking longer than before, but I hardly notice due to my excitement.

My mind soars, 'Wow. I cannot believe this is actually happening. She loves me, too.'

Finally, an answer rolls in.

Yes. I woke up in love with you a while ago.

My smile fades slightly.

Why didn't you tell me sooner?

I see that she is typing, I wait patiently.

I did not think that you would feel the same and I was hoping that you would say it first.

I let out a small laugh to surround my whisper, "Me too, babe. Me too."

CHAPTER TWENTY-FOUR:

My mind begins to fire with thoughts as I am awoken by the blare of my phone.

My squinted vision informs me that it is Victoria.

Do you want to go with me?

I smirk to myself as confusion overtakes my mind, giving her enough time to type another message.

I am taking you somewhere. It is a surprise.

I can feel the vibrations of a laugh slip past my throat.

I would love to. When?

Her mind is captured by our conversation, replying faster than normal.

Right now. Are you ready?

I read the first two words as I jump out of bed trying to compose a message as I walk towards the closet.

Yes. Now, sounds great :)

The morning process feels like it cannot be over fast enough. I nearly trip as I walk into my open, closet door. I regain my structure as I throw on a messy assembly of clothes. I can feel a small drop of toothpaste against my right, upper lip as I am making my way towards the door.

I pause before opening the barrier that separates me from her world. I give myself a moment to wipe away the stain on my mouth and head out the entryway.

The blazing lights blind my pathway allowing me to see nothing beyond the intense rays through my squinted vision.

I am relieved to make it to the other side of the illumination, taking a deep inhale, I search the parking lot for Victoria.

It does not take me long to spot her vehicle sitting in the spot, positioned in an uneven placement. I smirk at her driving, everything about this woman is intriguing to me.

The weight of my figure falls into the soft fabric that lines her passenger seat. My head leans in her direction giving our line of vision a chance to meet.

I feel the heat of our energy rising to the surface of my cheeks causing me to look away to avoid acknowledgement.

I feel the warmth of the back of her right-hand brush against the side of my face. The sensation of her skin rubbing along mine, sends a current of comfort to wash over me.

Her voice breaks the silent air around us, "Are you ready to go?"

I allow the weight of my head to bob forward in response. It does not take us long to get to the destination, I do not know much yet about how today is going to play out, she has no intention of relaying any details about the agenda. The only thing I am sure of is that we are in Dallas which is roughly forty-five minutes outside of where she lives.

I find myself peering out the window, enjoying the scenery of the downtown atmosphere. The curb side parking spot we land, is not too far from where she wants to take me.

She does some small touch ups on her make-up in the visor mirror before pushing the action of us actually getting out of the car.

I allow her to lead me down the sidewalk, in the direction of which we just came from. She guides me to a small, coffee shop that I normally would not have entered on my own.

The entire front of the shop is converted into a bookstore, with multiple tables that hold a large group of people scattered along the area in a careless spree. The back formation has an exit that leads out onto a patio space, the inside is much more crowded due to the coffee bar being in this area.

I am unsure of why she brought me in here, I am trying to get a clear look at the surroundings, when she takes us to the stools to have a seat.

Our experience in the shop is a great time, we hop out of the door and onto the next adventure, making sure to check out all of the whimsical shops that line the streets as we make our way back to the car after a long, but fulfilling day.

My right-hand brushes against her left, my eyes jump towards her face to see that she is already looking at me, smiling.

I take a few more steps before we get to into the cabin. The pound of both doors shutting, rings through my ears.

Her right, index finger glides over the start button allowing the vehicle to come to life.

We do not pull out into the road to continue home. Instead, we find ourselves sitting in the silence of our own minds.

I find myself secretly admiring her again, 'She is beautiful. Everything about her is perfect to me. I only wish I knew what she is thinking, what feelings are racing through her body, that she never tells me about?'

I lean the upper-half of my body forward, placing my right palm against her thigh. I slowly move my hand in a forward movement, towards her torso. Her figure reacts to my motions by matching each one back to me.

The next thing I know, she allows me to drip love from my fingertips and lips against her form while we drive home.

My hand rests in hers as she parks allowing me to get out of the car, "Thank you for taking me today. I always have such a great time with you."

Victoria smiles gently, "It is never enough time together."

CHAPTER TWENTY-FIVE:

I feel my mind being pulled out of a hazy fog, onto the sound of my phone going off. I look at the screen through blurred vision, seeing that it is ten o'clock in the morning on December eleventh and the person calling is, Victoria.

The groggy scratch of my voice sails through the phone, "Hello, beautiful."

Her uplifted tone sails into my mind, "Hello there. How are you?"

I nod my head slightly, "I am good. How are you, angel?"

A deep-rooted sigh leaves her chest, "I am fine. Do you want to go to the salon and hang out with me today?"

The weight of my head falls forwards slightly, "I would love to."

Her voice trails quickly out into the air, "Great! I will see you soon. Come by, whenever you want."

Even though she has given me no time frame. I know I want to get there as soon as possible.

I breeze through my morning routine, making a few stops on the way to see her.

I am inside of one of the shops, when I feel the sharp vibration of a text trying to consume my attention.

Where are you?

I am able to sense the warmth rising inside of me, seeing that it is from Victoria.

I type back quickly, heading out the door.

On my way. See you soon.

Before I exit the application, another charge of words come in.

Go to the back door.

I nod my head once in understanding with myself, sliding the device into my front pocket.

The brisk breeze of the winter wind cuts through my skin as I gather my things and head towards the entrance.

Victoria opens the door, revealing that someone else is occupying the space with her.

I find my face flush with embarrassment while her and one of the hairstylists stare at me.

I forcibly clear my throat, extending my arms out, away from my form. I present to her a glass casing that holds three, red roses and a small, non-fat latte.

She smiles, but I realize I have just made a mistake when I see the confusion and concern on the other girl's face.

Victoria takes the items, turning to walk further into the space.

They invite me into the awkward situation further. I am littered with the overpowering urge to pull my collar away from my throat so I can breathe.

It does not take long for the tension to push the woman out of Victoria's office.

I step towards her slightly, the guilt in my voice causes the words to shake, "I am so sorry. I had no idea someone else was in here."

Her head shifts slightly, "What?"

My mind sparks in confusion, "I am sorry that I brought you coffee and flowers. I did not know that she was in here. I know you said you did not want anyone to know."

She remains relaxed, "Oh, right. Do not stop doing something for me because of someone else. I do not care who knows as long as my family and friends do not."

I feel myself slipping further into my mind, 'I am not sure what I am supposed to do now. She said before no one can know, now some people can. I do not want to make her feel pressured to tell anyone, but I also do not want to do the wrong thing and it hurt her.'

My thoughts are broken by Victoria, placing her hand on my shoulder, "Are you okay?"

The presence of her touch, sends a current of peace to rush over me, "Yes."

We hold eye contact, when she breaks the silence, "Thank you for coming to hang out with me."

An uncontrollable smile melts against my mouth, "It is my pleasure."

Her smile remains as her thoughts continue, "Thank you for the flowers and the coffee, I really like them."

A brief silence flashes by as she continues, "Also, I have a question."

I feel the structure of my head fall to the right, "What's that?"

Her mouth twitches slightly, speaking in a softer flow, "Why do you call me, 'angel'?"

A nearly invisible laugh tries to escape the chamber of my throat, "I grew up to believe that we all have an angel. Someone who god made just for me. Someone that he would let me spend the rest of my life with. I believe he sent me you."

She pushes her head into a slight nod, "Interesting."

Her body language shifts, she pulls her body away from me, "I do not know if we are going to work."

I feel the cranks in my mind spin out of control as panic floods my mind, "What? Why not?"

Her eyes drop down towards the floor, "I have my reasons. I guess, we will just have to wait and see what happens. I can't make any promises."

I sit up slightly, "Is this something we can talk about?"

Her focus remains held on something else in the room as she speaks, "Not right now, no. I think that I just need some time to think. I will talk to you later."

I nod my head firmly, respecting her wishes as I turn to walk out the door. Part of my heart remains there with her, I find myself hoping that it will be enough for her.

It does not take me long to jump in the car and hit the road, the vibration of my cellular hitting against the plastic console grabs my attention.

On the other end of the phone, I can hear Victoria sobbing, "My niece just passed away."

I feel like the entire world has just been sucked dry of all the air currents as my heart aches for the pain she must be feeling, "I am so sorry for your loss do you need anything?"

Her tone breaks, "No. I will call you later."

I sigh deeply allowing the silence of the ride home to carry my thoughts, 'I feel so guilty. There has to be something I can do, even if it is just to be there for her. I feel this intense urge to turn around and go back to the salon, just to hold her, but then again, everyone handles death differently, she might want to just be alone right now with her thoughts. I do not want to impose, but not doing anything is torture.'

I have been at home now for nearly an hour, I think I am about to wear a hole in the rug from so much pacing. I cannot help it, my mind is too concerned about her to be able to relax. I try to distract my mind by walking around my living room like a caged lion, but my attention keeps drifting towards my home screen, ensuring that I did not accidentally miss a call from her.

Finally, I hear the phone ring, my heart nearly jumps out of my chest as I lunge towards the device, "Hello?"

Her tone is now heavy with pain, but I cannot hear any tears trying to break through her voice, "I want a drink."

I move my head towards my watch, seeing that it is now nearly six at night, "Okay. Where do you want to go?"

Exhaustion rings through her words, "It does not matter. Anywhere that has alcohol will work."

I nearly trip over my tongue trying to get out a response, "Okay. Meet me at the bar down the street. Drive safe."

I do not get a reply, other than the canceling tone of the phone call coming to an end.

I make it to the spot of destination faster than ever. I think I was going twenty over the speed limit, I just wanted to get to her and see if she was going to be okay. I needed to see her in person to fully believe it.

I find myself fidgeting with the papers in my car while I await her arrival. Finally, I see the blurred color of her paint pass the side of my vision to the right.

I greet her outside of the car with a tight hug, before I lead her in silence towards the restaurant.

We are seated in a booth next to the bar almost immediately greeted by a waiter.

Victoria speaks before he even has a chance to ask us what we want, "I want a mimosa."

He nods once in understanding before turning his attention towards me, "Vodka and lemonade."

He disappears from our table just as quickly as he showed earlier.

She begins to talk about her niece, sharing stories of her life and expressing the pain she is feeling inside.

A few more drinks are brought to the table, taking her sadness and allowing her to laugh at memories, before a thought shoots through her head, "I cannot drink anymore. Will you take me to your house, until I sober up? I do not want my daughter to see me like this."

I nod, guiding her figure towards my car that is now hidden under the dark shadows of the night.

We slip into the cabin with ease, the overhead light allows me to get a glimpse of her smile in my direction as she gives me a slow kiss.

I inform her to put on her seat belt while I pull out of the parking spot, heading towards the house.

I get her coffee upon our arrival, her stay consists of talking about her memories and thoughts further. I am thankful that she trusts me enough to be able to share her mind so freely with me.

Once she is sober enough to drive, she asks me to take her back to her car. I do as she wishes, even though I would do anything to be able to stay with her all night just in case she might need something.

It hurts my heart to see her leave, but I knew it was what I had to do.

Before she fully gets in her car, she stops me, "You will go to the funeral with me, right?"

I nod my head, "Of course. I would never make you go through that alone. I love you, I am here."

She gives me a fast, fake smile, "I love you, too."

CHAPTER TWENTY-SIX:

A few weeks have now passed since Victoria had to go through the loss of her loved one. You can tell she still carries the pain, but she knows that you have to continue on. I find that she is a fighter, always going through life like a bulldozer, not allowing too many things to phase her, but not being truly happy, is one thing she doesn't let up on easily.

The dial on my phone is busy with Victoria.

She speaks to me about my day briefly, before changing the subject, "What are you doing on Christmas?"

My eyes rise slightly as I scan the invisible calendar in my mind, finding that there is only five days till the holiday, "Nothing much. Why, what's going on?"

A small sigh leaks from her lips, catching my attention, "I do not know what I am going to do with my daughter. I want to take her somewhere that she can experience Christmas."

I pull the structure of my bottom lip into my teeth as I rack my mind over the idea slightly before allowing it to consume the air, "I could have Christmas at my house and you guys can come over if you want."

She hums loudly in my ear as she re-thinks the idea, "Okay well, I will let you know soon if that is something we want to do. I will talk to you later. Okay, thanks. Bye."

I gently place the phone down on the coffee table, playing over the possible plan of having people over for Christmas. I have not done this in years, I hope everything goes smoothly.

The next day, I get a phone call from Victoria saying that her and her daughter are going to come over to my house for Christmas. That was this morning, now here I am a few hours later looking for some gifts that they would enjoy and getting everything ready for the meal.

I can feel the anxiety of doing everything with perfection is beginning to take a toll on me and it is only the first day.

I try my hardest the rest of the week to get everything perfect.

The day of Christmas was a good day in my book, everyone seemed to have a good time. I am really blessed to have been able to spend it with them, there was nowhere else in any form of reality that I would have rather been.

I find myself finally being able to sit down and rest on the couch after the long day. It is a good kind of tired but still, looking at the pile of dishes that I yet have to do makes my skin crawl.

I exhale loudly allowing the weight of my head to fall towards my darkened phone screen. I get lost in the colorful lights on the walls reflecting off of the surface. Suddenly, my mind is brought to life by the small, yellow LED light flashing on the very tip of the display.

My heart begins to pound sharply, knowing that I must have missed a notification from Victoria while I was cleaning.

My eyes quickly scan the words in a sweeping motion.

Thank you so much for doing that for her. I think she had a good time.

I smirk to myself, throwing the weight of my structure in a heap of exhaustion as I type back.

*Of course, anytime. I am glad she enjoyed it.
I hope you did, too. Good night, beautiful. I
love you. Sweet dreams, sweetheart.*

CHAPTER TWENTY-SEVEN:

I feel the sleep in my eyes shift as they begin to flutter open. The small rays of light that are peaking through the blinds ignite my mind to reality. I reach for my phone trying to identify the time, it does not take me long to see that it is seven in the morning on January seventh.

The new year brings new things. I am still trying to figure out what exactly happened to me and where I am. This version of reality seems so familiar, yet at the same time I feel like an outcast.

My mind trails off to Victoria. I wish I could see her today. It never fails, no matter what kind of mood I am in seeing her automatically makes everything a hundred times better.

My chest releases a small gust of air, 'I know that with her starting this new job and everything going on in her life at the moment, things are hard. I feel guilty when I tell her I miss her, but I cannot help it. She has become a bigger part of my life then even she realized in such a short amount of time. It felt like a whirl wind, but through the spinning, I realized that there is no one else in this world I'd rather be in this situation with than her.'

The new career shift happened due to personal reasons, issues that most should not be discussed with me. I try not to pry too much, I feel like it is not my place then on the other hand, I feel like minding my own business is a horrible thing for a partner to do.

I take a deep breath trying to convince myself that I am in fact doing the right thing by her, 'It is okay, Sam. If she wanted you to know, she would tell you.'

I try to dive into work, hoping that it will be enough to distract my mind from worrying about Victoria. To my disapproval, the workload only stares back at me as my brain is unable to do anything other than think about her.

I sigh gently, the brush of air that lingers over my bottom lip is soothing.

The job that she has switched to, makes her go out of the city, roughly two hours from where we live. Right now, she is currently training which makes me feel a little safer, but not fully. The training is with her ex-boyfriend and I am trying to keep a positive mindset.

The phone in my front pocket begins to go off, informing me that she is attempting to get a hold of me through a vocal expression, "Hey, babe. How are you?"

I cannot hold back the goofy grin that wants to form against my lips, "I am well. How is work?"

I can hear the dissatisfaction rushing along her tone, "It is fine. The drive is long, but the people are nice. I think this is something I could really enjoy doing. I have to go now, but I just wanted to call and tell you that I love you. We will speak later. I love you."

I nod my head in understanding as I nearly trip over my tongue trying to get the words to escape, "Okay, talk soon. I love you."

The echo of my voice is still running through the air as she hits the end button.

I feel my body relax under the notion that she is in fact okay. I am glad she called. Although, it does seem like she is trying to convince herself to like this job. I hope it is something that grows on her, she deserves better than to work at a bad job.

The call of my job begins to grow far too loud for me to ignore. I find myself being able to get lost in the mounds of papers, waiting for the phone to alert me of my next break.

CHAPTER TWENTY-EIGHT:

The day is now Thursday and I find myself waking up to a heavy headache. I hurry to the bathroom, rifling through the cabinets, looking for a form of aspirin to kill the pain. I nearly toss the bottle to the ground after emptying out a grand total of the remaining six pills and popping them into my mouth.

A small illumination of light stretching down the hall towards my bathroom, is brought to my attention from the source of the living room. I quickly make my way through the darkness trying to find the reason behind this. It does not take me more than a matter of seconds to learn it is from my phone. It is trying to inform me that I missed a call from her.

I immediately dial her phone, it rings three times before she answers in a joyful tone, "Did I wake you?"

The playfulness of her tone causes me to let out a small laugh, "No, you did not. I was already awake. I was just in the bathroom."

Her response is quick with less pep in every word, "Oh, I see. Well, what are you doing later?"

I shake my head gently, thinking about the things left to do on my list, "Nothing much. Why?"

The tone of her voice shifts back to a happier state, finding out that I am not doing anything else, "Good. I wanted to know if you would like to hang out. I can come over if you would like?"

She asks as if she already knows the answer, yet a large part of her remains unsure.

I feel an intense need to reply back in a comforting voice, "Of course, I would love for you to come over. We can have coffee. When do you want to do that?"

Particles of her breath hit against the speaker, "Would now be okay? I really want to see you."

My chest begins to fill with a slight jump of anticipation, "Now would be great."

I throw the phone down on the counter, running the flat surface of my hands against the structure of my face as I rack my mind for an idea, 'It is okay. I can just run next door and see if anyone has milk. I never carry it in the house, it makes me ill, but I have heard her say before that she does not like my creamer. If I go right now and hurry, I should be able to beat her back.'

I nearly jump out of my skin, running towards the counter to scoop up the keys. The silver ridged pieces clink together as I make my way to the car.

The transaction is much faster than I was thinking it was going to be in my head.

I am back home with time to spare, I did not even waste three minutes on the clock.

I walk into the apartment with a more relaxed stroll, quickly making my way to the kitchen to start the pot of coffee. I would have made it before, but I know that she does not like when it tastes burnt.

My mind is triggered by the last thought, shooting my mind back to an old memory, 'It is of Victoria. She is telling me, "I feel like you never are paying attention to me. You are always all over. Everywhere but here." I feel a smile creep across my face as I think, 'You have no idea how I hang on to every word that leaves those lips.'

My thoughts are shattered by a knock at the door, three times in a soft collision. I rush towards the door, slowing myself down just enough so she would not be able to hear my excited, pounding feet smacking against the entry tiles. A large gust of air is pulled into my lungs as I drag the weight of the door towards my figure.

I am greeted with the always beautiful view of my lovely girlfriend, standing in the threshold.

She greets me with a gentle smile, "Hi."

My arms extend away from my form, stepping into a long hug. I can feel the placement of her hand on my back, moving in small circles before she pats twice. This informs me that she has had enough for now. I let her go due to our unspoken conversation.

I urge her to have a seat on the couch while I go to get her coffee.

I carefully walk in her direction with two nearly full cups in my grasp.

I pass her the one with milk, "Here you go, angel."

She smiles slightly, raising the glass towards her mouth, letting only in a small amount, "This is very hot."

Her body is pushed forwards allowing her to place the coffee cup down on the table.

She uses her right hand to pat against the cushion, "Sit next to me."

I allow my body to follow the command of her soothing voice, I find myself sitting less than three inches away from her.

She turns her head slightly, admiring my face, "You have circles under your eyes, you are not getting enough sleep."

I raise my eyebrows slightly, "Yeah, I know. I just can't sleep."

She reaches for her cup, hoping that by now it has cooled down enough to drink, "Are you okay?"

I nod my head once, "I just miss you."

She smiles, pulling me closer into her arms, "I know that now with this new job, we do not get to see each other as much as we would like, but we will figure something out. We are in front of one another, right now. We just have to make the most of every moment together. Really make them count."

I can feel the racing pound of her heart hitting against my inner ear as I listen to it escalate.

A strong feeling of paranoia rushes over my mind, "We are okay, right?"

Her vision shifts slightly, "Yes. Why are you asking that?"

I release a falsified laugh, "I just get weird thoughts in my head sometimes. Sorry, I do not know why it happens."

She nods her head as if to tell me she understands, but the look of concern on her face makes me nervous.

Another question slips out of my throat before I even have a chance to fully process it, "Are you happy with me?"

She seems taken aback by my question, the rain of guilt begins to fall around me as my shoulders slouch under her response, "Yes. Why are you asking me these things?"

The weight of her voice seems heavier than before, "Are you mad at me?"

A long sigh is released from the passages of her nose, "I am not mad at you. I just do not get you. You are fine then one minute you just get really weird. Do you realize that I have to mentally prepare myself to even stand to be around you? That is why I do not stay long, it just becomes too much. You are too much for me to handle sometimes."

I exhale deeply, feeling my figure drop about twenty levels into a bad place, 'I do not know why I am like this. I just feel very bad. I do not know if it is what I went through. Maybe, I should try to explain it.'

My eyes shift in her direction, my voice cracks as it tries to come to life, "I am sorry. I did not mean to upset you. I think this might just be a form of PTSD from my past relationships. They were always mad at me or when I did something wrong, they had to make sure to make a big deal about how I cannot do anything right. They told me that they didn't want to be around me. Certain things are like triggers and send my mind to a very bad place. They used to do and say things like what you just said to me."

I feel a shift in her persona, from confusion to anger.

I can feel the rough vibrations of her tone bouncing against my mind, "I am not them. I am nothing like them. Do not compare me to people in your past because I am nothing like those people. You know what—I have had enough, right now. I am just going to go. I have stuff I have to do. See—this is exactly what I mean. You get into these weird moods and I do not know what to do. I feel like I cannot even talk to you without hurting your feelings."

I feel my mind search for my voice as I want to beg and scream— anything to get her to stay and not leave, but the only thing my chest will allow to come out is a silent whisper, "Okay."

She stretches out her arms to me in a comforting manner, "Come here, babe. Lay down with me. Cuddle with me, let's just hold each other and enjoy the time we are together. Everything is okay, we are going to be alright."

The sound of her heart begins to fade as she moves gently underneath me. She is not the biggest fan of cuddling, so when she does allow us to, it means more to me than she could ever even begin to imagine.

A wall of regret from our earlier fight starts to flood my mind as I see her advancing towards the door, she turns slightly, "Are you going to walk me out to the car?"

I nod twice in a rapid pace, following her out into the gloomy skyline. The air is filled with nothing more than our silence, I hold the structure of the door while she slides into the seat.

Her eyes meet mine, I cannot help but to say what is on my mind, "I love you."

She drops her sight towards the dash, "Okay, well. I will talk to you later."

I feel my heart sink slightly, watching her drive further away from my grasp.

I sigh loudly, making sure I know how disappointed I am with myself. I drag my weight into the confines of my home, placing the structure of my messy figure on the couch.

Where I sit, completely lost in thoughts, 'I hate that I am like this. I do not want to lose her. I have no idea what is wrong with me. I just want to be as perfect as I can for her and it seems like every time I open my mouth, I say something wrong. I feel stuck. She means so much to me, I would do anything to make sure she stays mine. I just wish I could stop making her upset. I fear that one day, I really will be too much for her like she says and she will give up on me.'

Just the lone thought causes a stream of silent tears to fall from my vision, 'I have to start watching myself more carefully. I cannot make any more mistakes, I feel as though I have already made too many. I hate fighting with her, it makes me image what swallowing a knife must feel like. Hopefully, I get better at this.'

CHAPTER TWENTY-NINE:

A few days have now passed since I have last seen Victoria. Thankfully, we have still remained in contact through messages and phone calls.

I feel like we have gotten past the episode and can continue on with our relationship.

She said she was supposed to come over today. I am excited that I will be able to see her. It rips me apart inside to know that we had a fight three days ago and I have not been able to hold her in my arms since. I think that today is going to be a good day for us.

Not too much time has passed since I last looked at the clock, informing me that it was close to noon, the time she was supposed to be here.

My eyes dance towards the phone, when I hear a soft knock upon the wooden flesh of the panel.

My mind fires with thoughts, 'She is right on time. I like that.'

I open the barrier that currently is between us. She stands in the threshold, staring at me with glowing eyes, that look like small puddles of amber under the light.

I feel the weight of my head pull into a firm shake.

Her attention forces her head to lean to the right, "What is funny?"

The smirk that is currently growing along my face is unable to be contained, "Nothing. You are just beautiful."

She stares at me as if she is shocked or maybe even confused, for a reason I cannot understand.

Suddenly as if she is being pulled out of a deep thought.

She speaks in an unenthusiastic tone, "Well, thank you."

I pull my lips into a fake smile, "You are welcome. Do you want to sit down? Would you like something to drink? I have water or coffee."

Her response remains short, "No. No, thank you. I am good. Here, come here. Sit with me."

I release a strong breath of air, carrying my form over by her. She positions her body on an angle allowing herself to face me.

I try to lean in to give her a hug, but she places her palms in the joints of my shoulders. The small amounts of resistance I feel from her causes me to back off immediately.

I sit with a puzzled look of distress riding along my face, "What is wrong?"

She shakes her head gently, "Nothing. Nothing. I just wanted to look at you."

I feel the heat of her gaze crawl against my flesh while my mind begins to run at a hundred miles an hour, 'I wonder why she did that? Maybe, I am hugging her too much. Other people have told me before that sometimes I am too clingy. Or, maybe it is something else. Maybe, she does not feel the same way towards me anymore. Maybe, she is losing her feelings for me.'

The current of my thoughts are broken by her voice crackling to life, "You are very attractive."

I feel the stain of red, run against my face, "Thank you."

She stretches her arm out towards me, "I just want to stare at you."

I feel my right hand extend towards the top of hers, she does not react to my gesture until she pulls it out from underneath my weight. She uses the fingers of that hand to act as a comb, running her hand along my hair.

I sigh gently, "You can stare at me."

My vision drops slightly, "Babe, can I have a hug?"

She nods once as I pull her into an embrace, it does not take more than a few seconds for the half-hug is broken by her pulling away from me.

The weight of my mind begins to crush my thoughts as they try to convince me that she does not feel the same about me like she once did.

CHAPTER THIRTY:

I guess, the weather here in the book or wherever the hell I am, is just as unpredictable as real life. A random storm blew in through mid-day, hitting all local areas up to four hours away.

While watching the news, I feel an intense fear overtake the inside of my form, 'I hope she is going to be okay in the snow.'

I place my phone beside me, making sure the switch is set to loud, just in case. I do not want to miss her call because I am working or distracted.

I find myself staring at the half-blank page allowing my vision to scan each one. Yet, my mind is not able to process what is supposed to happen next in the story.

A deep sigh is pushed from my nasal canals, pulling my form into a full stance as I begin to pace the floor. I allow the words of the Meteorologist to consume me.

Finally, the air is broken by the sound of Victoria trying to reach me.

I answer with a tone full of restrained distress, "Hello, are you okay?"

She sighs slightly, "Yes, sorry. I just got home—"

The expressions of her voice are drowned out by my mind decompressing, 'I am so glad that she is okay. I was so worried. I thought I was going to jump out of my skin. I have never had that kind of anxiety over someone else before. This is new. I am so glad she is okay.'

I can finally feel like I can breathe again.

My thoughts have now slowed greatly, I continue to listen harder as she speaks freely, "You know, I was thinking about how Valentine's day is coming up"

A smirk rises to my mouth, "Yes. I have been thinking about that, too."

Her mind races, "Well, you continue to think about that. I am going to get a few things done here around the house."

My now relaxed state is flooding through my vocal cords, "Okay, angel. I will get something together. Talk soon. Bye."

She clicks the end button, slightly cutting off her good-bye speech.

My eyes close gently as I tip my head back, hoping to organize my thoughts. I light a cigarette to slowly engulf the room with a misty smoke as I type her a text.

Hey, beautiful. I just wanted you to know, my feelings for you grow every single day. The intensity of them, surprises me. I have never felt so true, so strongly about anyone. Today, I was so concerned when I did not know if you were going to be okay or not. I am glad you are okay. I am so thankful that you are mine.

It takes roughly two hours before I get a reply.

I smirk gently at the response.

I was thinking about Valentine' s day and I have an idea.

This time, the conversation progresses much faster.

What is it?

My fingers become numb from holding onto my phone so tightly, the only thing that brings me closer to her when we are apart.

You know how we both always talk about being able to spend a night together? We should go to a hotel.

The chat bubble at the bottom of the screen appears.

Yes. That would be nice. We can meet up on the thirteenth, I already have plans on the fourteenth for a work thing, I will be with an ex as my cover. Then we can just figure out what to do when we meet up.

I feel a surge of energy rush through my body as my mind soars, 'I cannot wait to be able to hold her in my arms all night.'

I feel the weight of a sigh leave my lips, 'I know I am supposed to be her secret, but I also think I am becoming jealous of her covers. This is not good. I have to get over this, now if I want our relationship to work.'

CHAPTER THIRTY-ONE:

The weight of my head falls forward, pulling me back to reality. I look around my surroundings to see that I must have fallen asleep doing work last night. I could not help it. I was so excited about today, my mind would just not allow me to fall asleep naturally.

My attention gets shot to the screen of my phone, informing me that it is around seven in the morning on February the thirteenth.

My mind plays through the events of the day. I quickly jump on my schedule, getting everything prepared. I want this to be absolutely perfect, she deserves only the best.

Once I get all of my surprises set up, I take a small moment to rest before my phone rings, it is Victoria, "Hello, beautiful."

The sound of her reply is soothing, "Hi there, babe. I just got finished with work. Where do you want me to meet you?"

My smile is unshakable, "I will text you the address. It's the Silent Night Hotel. Call when you get here."

Before she has a fair chance to say anything, my anticipation hangs up the line.

I immediately jump into my texts, typing in the address of the hotel.

My mind is locked in a daydream state as I sit in patience, awaiting her arrival.

The vibrating pattern of my phone alerts me that she is here, "Hello. Are you outside?"

Her voice echoes through the phone, "No. I am in the lobby. Where are you?"

I try to keep my tone controlled, "In room two. If you are staring at the check in desk. Take a left down the hall, climb the stairs and it will be the only room up there. You cannot miss it. Tell me when you get here."

I am able to detect the confusion lining her tone, "Okay? Why?"

My mind is not good at keeping secrets.

I attempt to alter the direction of her thoughts, "Are you on the second floor, yet?"

She sighs, "Yes. Just got on the floor. Now what?"

A nervous laugh slips past my lips, "Take a right, it is the door all the way at the end, left side of the hallway. Just walk in, it is open."

I hear the line go dead as the doorknob begins to rattle. She opens the dark stained wooden barrier between us with caution.

Her eyes light up slightly as she entered into a dim, candle lit room. The floor and the one bed are draped in red, rose petals. On the right side of the bed, sits a large, garden tub with fully working jets on the side and bottom. It too, is sprawled with flower decorations and outlined in flickering lights that burn in the scent of vanilla.

I am currently standing in nothing, but my underwear, holding a glass of champagne in my right hand which is extended out towards her.

She looks overwhelmed by the room.

She gently takes the glass from my hand, "Can I sit down?"

I nod once, guiding her into the chair, "Are you okay?"

She takes a small sip of the drink, "Yes. This is just, wow. I did not expect this."

I tilt my head to the right, "What did you expect?"

Her head shakes slightly, "I guess, I am just so used to guys only thinking about one thing."

My heart burns for her as I kiss the top of her head, "Do you want to get in the tub?"

A bright smile engulfs her face, "Yes."

I laugh as I watch her slowly undress, she peers up at me, "Do not watch me get in."

A goofy grin plasters along my face as I cover my eyes with fingers, like a set of blinds. The sound of water droplets crashing against the sides of the tub, informs me that it is now safe for me to look.

With the majority of her body covered with bubbles, the only thing I am able to see clearly is from her neck, to the last-minute option of putting her hair up in a messy formation.

She extends her right arm slowly towards me, "Can I have my glass of champagne, now?"

I nod, walking over to the ice bucket to be able to top off her glass.

She smiles as I hand her a bowl of freshly cut strawberries, covered in a dust of salt. Using her right, index finger and thumb, she picks through the mound. Almost as if she is trying to find the perfect one. Finally, she places the fruity delicacy into her mouth.

The structure of her eyes widen, "This is my favorite."

An uncontrollable smile leaks from my soul, "Yeah, I know. So, cutie are you enjoying it?"

She moves her body closer to the edge, "I am not cute. I do not want to be cute. I want to be sexy and powerful."

My eyebrows rise slightly, "You are all three."

A larger than normal smile shines against me, "Get in."

I settle down in the wavy water, after discarding my items of clothing allowing my body to relax under the warmth hidden in the droplets.

The night goes a lot better than I thought it would. She absolutely adores the tub. I think I am going to have a hard time getting her out. We have been in here now, long enough to finish an entire medium, thin crust, cheese pizza, garlic bread and two bottles of champagne.

My mind begins to reel with an idea, "Do you want a massage?"

It does not take long for her to jump out of the tub and onto the bed. Red rose petals shower down around the front of the room as she pulls the blankets back.

Once she seems settled into bed, laying on her stomach. I take one of the candles that is slightly different than the others. The wax is vanilla in flavor and makes a great oil. I hold the warm, tin container above her form allowing only a thin stream of cream-colored wax to bead up along her skin. Her spine arches slightly under the sensation.

In the middle of her massage, she flips the structure of her body. Now, I am straddling the front of her form, being careful not to put too much weight on her.

She gently rests the surface of her palms around the structure of my face, pulling me towards her as she whispers into my mouth, "I want you to love me."

A few hours later, I am unable to feel anything other than the rapid pound of my heart. I attempt to slow my breathing, looking towards Victoria. She has her right forearm flung over her head as her eyes remain shut.

I find myself speaking in a soft manner as if I am fearful of disturbing her, "Are you tired, angel?"

She nods her head slowly, glancing towards the clock, "Oh, no. It is almost midnight."

A giant pause forms in her thoughts, "I am so sorry. I cannot stay. I do not know what to tell the kids."

I try to hide my internal feelings as deeply as I can, "It is okay."

I feel a lump beginning to build in my throat as my mind explodes, 'Maybe, I am wrong. Maybe, she does not feel the same way as me. Maybe, something else is going on.'

My rapidly declining thoughts are shattered by Victoria, "Will you walk me out?"

I quickly hop around the room, throwing on a pair of pants and a white t-shirt.

She stops before exiting the room, scanning it over in a fast sweep, stopping as she makes eye contact with me, "You are cute."

A goofy grin slips past my barriers, "Are you ready? Do you have everything?"

She nods her head once as I lead her towards the vehicle.

Before she gets in all the way, she pauses to give me a gentle kiss, "Thank you so much for tonight. I really enjoyed it. I will talk to you in the morning."

I stand in the spot she just left, watching the red glow of her taillights disappearing further out of reach every second. I quickly reach into my pocket, retrieving a pack of smokes. The burning amber reminds me of the taillights of her car. I quickly toss it to the concrete, watching the explosion of fiery sparks erupt upon impact.

The lobby is engulfed with multiple vending machines. I stroll over to get myself a well needed energy drink. On my walk back to the room, I had to pass the worker, who not only saw how the whole night unfolded, but also checked me in. I nod my head towards him slightly trying to remain calm, walking back to the room.

Once inside, my eyes are forced to readjust to the dim lights. A deep sigh is pushed out of my chest as I start to clean up the room, putting everything away the best I can. My eyes glance over towards the gifts she gave me.

A large, light brown teddy bear that is holding a tight grip on a red flush, heart shaped pillow, with white letters, 'I love you' and a rose bush. One of which she wants me to plant, tend to it every day. So as the rose grows, so will our love.

The mental exhaustion of the day has me worn out to the extent of no going back.

I allow the weight of my body to plop down on the bed in a sitting placement, 'I wonder if she was ever planning on staying. I feel like there might have been a different reason she left. Maybe, I did something.'

I give my mind a minute to ponder on the thoughts as I fumble with a rose petal, 'Then again, maybe, it was just about sex. She did say when she got here, she thought that was what would happen for being at the hotel, but then again, that does not make any sense. Maybe, I am just freaking out over something for no reason.'

The weight of my head falls into my palms as tears drain down, 'I am so scared that she does not feel the same way about me. I am madly in love with her and it is amazing and wonderful, everything I have ever dreamed of. Yet, her feelings for me remain unknown and messy.'

My internal voice saddens along with my mind, 'But, I never know what she is thinking or what she is feeling about me. Maybe, she is just a really good actress. No, Sam. Calm down. Just talk to her in the morning, everything will be okay.'

CHAPTER THIRTY-TWO:

It has been a normal day, we are still in February. I feel like this year has been going by so slow. I have not done a whole lot of anything, besides work today—like most days. Thankfully, I enjoy what I do for a living. It is roughly around eight at night.

I take a deep breath allowing my mind to drift off towards Victoria. It has been a few hours since we last spoke. Suddenly, I hear the phone blow up with a musical vibration set just for her.

My body reacts to the notification in a flash, "Hello."

Her concern leaks through the holes in the speaker, "Hey. So, my Dad had to go to the hospital. He had to get a stent put in. He is okay, everything will be okay. He will have to stay here in the hospital for a few days while they monitor him."

My head nods quickly as I retain all the information, "I am so sorry that happened. I am glad he is going to be okay. Do you need anything? Is there anything I can do?"

She releases a long sigh into the phone, "No. No, I am good. Thank you, though. I am just up here with my Mom. I do not want to leave her alone."

I exhale sharply trying to get the words to come out properly, "Okay, good. Well, if you need anything, let me know. I am here. Keep me updated."

Her voice cracks, "Okay, I love you. I will talk to you soon."

CHAPTER THIRTY-THREE:

A few days have now passed since I last seen Victoria, but we try our hardest to stay in touch other ways.

I allow my mind to run freely with my thoughts as I type a new message.

How do you feel about me?

With my brain trying to process every possible outcome of a reply, I try to bury my crazy hallucinations into my work.

Thankfully, this is one of the few times, the method is actually successful. My attention is shattered by the two-toned ring of her attempt to reach out to me.

I will tell you later when we are on the phone.

I sigh trying to piece my feelings together. I do not know what to think about her response. It could be anything, good or bad.

The rest of the day, I find myself drifting back towards her. My attempt to work has been officially declared pointless.

My focus shifts onto the phone buzzing against the glass surface of the table, it is Victoria.

My voice becomes engulfed with anxiety, "Hi, how are you?"

Before she even begins talking, I find myself analyzing her tone, hoping to be able to detect her mood.

A long gulp of air is released from her throat in a mutual manner, "I am good. Today was okay. Turns out, that I am getting a new boss. We are having a bet about if they are going to be attractive or not. I do not know much about them. I won't find out until tomorrow. This is all a good thing though because right now, the agency is crazy. It really needs someone to watch over it."

I feel the slight glimpse of a smile run over my face, "Good. I am glad to hear that things are going to get better."

A few days have now floated past since I have last initiated a meeting with her.

My mind guides the structure of my thumbs to craft a text.

I know I have been asking this a lot here lately, but I wanted to at least try. Do you want to go have a drink later?

Her answer is faster than I expected.

I am sorry, babe. I am just so exhausted. I do not want to do anything but go to bed after work.

I exhale sharply giving myself a moment to inhale all of the information.

Okay, babe. Don't worry. I understand.

A sense of relief floods through my brain, seeing that she replied with three heart symbols.

Roughly another week has now passed. The hustle of everyday life has caused us to still fail to have a proper face to face meeting.

The sound of the phone ringing, grabs my attention, it is her, "Hey."

I can hear the smile on her lips as she speaks, "Hi, babe. How are you?"

The waves of my voice attempt to match hers, "Great and yourself?"

A strong gust of air is pushed from her lungs, "Good. Just heading out to work. What about you? What are you going to do today?"

My tone comes out faster than I imagined, "I am working, too. Hey, I have a question. What are you doing later tonight?"

A long groan flows from the chamber of her throat, "I have no idea, yet. Why are you asking?"

I shake my head in a defensive manner, nearly forgetting that she is unable to see me, "I was just curious. I thought that since you did not have to work tomorrow. Maybe, we can have that drink tonight?"

A long, humming vibration occupies the space between us while she figures out what to say from here, "I do not know, babe. I do not know how I am going to feel. But we will try, okay?"

The weight of my head tips forwards, pushing the words out, "Okay, sounds great. Talk to you later. I hope you have an amazing day at work."

My body is being overtaken with the hope of being able to see her which allows me to get a hunk of things done in my job today.

I hear the muffled vibrations of my phone on the couch, "Hello?"

I am greeted with the high-pitched tone of my lover, "Hi, babe. How are you?"

I feel a surge of energy rush over me, "Great. Are you getting a lot done?"

She clarifies what her good mood already told me, "Yes! It has been an amazing day! I made so many collections already and it is only 1 p.m. I still have until 7p.m."

I feel a small chuckle come up my throat, "Good. I am so glad to hear that. I am proud of you."

Another burst of enthusiasm drains from her bottom lip, "And, guess what? We have to gather collections from small companies, too. We even have to collect from the bars. We are going to save one of them for the last one of the day. That way we can go in when we are finished working and have a drink."

I feel the impact of her words against me, not being able to give her a proper response, "Wow, that is really cool, babe."

While talking, I realize that I am doing the best I can to hold back any emotion that wants to slip through.

The tone of her voice shifts to irritation, "Are you okay? What is wrong?"

I shake my head as letters fall, "Nothing."

Her words become amplified, "Something is wrong. See, this is what I am always talking about. This is why I have to mentally prepare myself to be around you or even to talk to you on the phone. I just do not know how to handle you sometimes."

I clear my throat slightly, "I am sorry."

A rough breath is shot from her throat, "Do not be sorry. Just tell me what is wrong."

My mind puts up a flag, informing me not to tell her, but my heart wins every battle, "Fine. Okay, I will tell you. So, it really seems to hurt my feelings because I have been asking you for weeks now to go have a drink with me. When I ask, you always say one day or maybe sometime soon, when I am not so tired and it cannot be on a night where I worked all day. But, when your boss asks you, you are about to go then? Even on a work night."

The agitation in her form increases, "This again. How many times do I have to tell you? I do not like my boss. See, this is why I did not know if I wanted to be with you. You are so damn sensitive. You get upset over nothing; you are so immature. Damn. There, it is over. We can talk about it later."

I sigh into the dying line, 'Damn, is right. And, I thought I was confused before. Now, my mind feels like a huge puzzle that I am never destined to solve. I wish I could just figure out how she feels about me.'

I pause momentarily, thinking back on my previous attempts, 'She never gives me an actual answer. Even when I ask her directly, she always response with, 'We will talk later.' Yet, something always comes up and we never do. Part of me feels like she is trying to stall, the other half of me does not have any idea what is even going on. I just wish she would have been that excited to see me. I never see her now. This really has me questioning, does she even miss me when I am gone?'

CHAPTER THIRTY-FOUR:

I have been waking up here lately trying to keep the past where it belongs. We are only going to do that by us working together. It has been six days since I last got to hold her in my arms thankfully, that changes later today. I miss her, this visit is going to be really good.

The notification of an incoming call, "Hey, I am outside."

A rush of excitement shoots through my body, "Great. Come on in. The door is unlocked."

A heavy silence falls over me, seeing she ended the call prematurely. The moment she walks in the door, I feel the weight of my figure gliding towards her. I wrap her tightly in a hug, a powerful sense of peace always floods my soul when we are holding each other, but something about this day is different.

Within the first three seconds of the hug, I can feel her hands resting in my shoulders, pushing me away.

The feeling of her rejection causes my thoughts to run on edge, 'Wow, what did I do? One second, she wants to do nothing but love on me and now, I do not even get a decent hug?'

My thoughts are shifting as her voice enters my mind, "Can we sit?"

I nod my head once, following behind her as she sits on the couch.

She turns her body to face me, straightening out her back, "So, talk to me. What has all been going on?"

I feel my vision drop slightly, "Nothing, really. I just miss you."

I push the upper-half of my body forwards trying to lean in to kiss her. She does not allow me to advance any closer.

She pushes me backwards, "Babe. Here, just sit there and talk to me for a minute."

The entire structure of my figure melts into a negative sway.

A harsh bite to her tone, informs me that she has noticed it too, "See, why do you always have to get in these moods?"

My words crack like a whip against the airway, "I am not in any kind of mood. I just miss you."

She examines me as if trying to read my mind, "I do not think that is what's really going on with you."

The weight of my head pulls forwards slightly, "Really, I am not lying. I just wish we could spend more time together."

Her reply is less stiff than the last, "Why do you miss me? I am right here."

A notification on her phone, pulls her attention away from the topic of us.

My mind begins to barrel through a train of thoughts, 'Man, this has to be something more than just my paranoia. I really think that she is already getting tired of me. Maybe, I am not trying hard enough.'

The weight of my voice is drowned out by Victoria, clearing her throat, "Come here. Give me a hug. I know that we do not get to see each other as much as we want and I know that it is hard, but I am going to have to leave soon. I have some stuff I need to take care of. Will you walk me to my car?"

I nod my head in a slow motion, pulling myself towards the door. She slips into a settled position in her car faster than normal.

Once her back lights fully fade from my view, I find myself alone with nothing but my mind to keep me company, 'I am sitting here, day in and day out trying to solve this puzzle. I am trying so hard to understand what is going on. She keeps telling me that she is not like my exes, this information gives me comfort, but it is still hard. I feel like I do not know where I stand. One minute she tells me she does not care if other people know then I am nothing more than her 'best friend'. I feel like in some moments she really loves me then in others, it seems almost like torture when I go in for a hug. One point in our relationship, she wants to see me every day. Now, I see her once a week, every Thursday for an hour then she has to leave. One moment, she wants to make love to me for hours on end, the next thing I know, she hasn't shown me physical affection in over a month. I just do not know what to think anymore.'

CHAPTER THIRTY-FIVE:

Well, it's Thursday again. I feel like in the back of my mind, I solely live for the days that are spent with her. She is so much more than just my girlfriend, she is my best friend. I want nothing more than to make her the happiest woman in the world.

Something about today, it is beautiful weather in March. In my head, that means it is the perfect opportunity to have wine at the park.

I just got off the phone with Victoria not too long ago. She informed me that she was roughly ten minutes away.

My mind begins to race with the excitement of being able to see her. I rush out the front door, making sure to grab everything I need that was previously prepared in my black backpack.

I approach the drivers side window, with a goofy grin plastered along my face as I grip the right shoulder strap of the bag in a nervous manner.

Her vision squints sharply, "What are you doing?"

I can feel my voice deepen as I try to hide my plan, "I am kidnapping you. Come on, get in my car."

A flash of irritation rushes over her, "Why?"

I shrug my shoulders slightly, "It will be fun. Come on."

A harsh gust of air is pushed from her lungs, "Fine. Come on, let's go then."

I push a breath of defeat from my chest, 'Why can't I do anything right?'

The ride to the hidden gem is wrapped in silence. Once the car is safely parked, we advance quickly outside.

I lead her towards a lone picnic table. It holds a perfect view of the lake below. I hand her a glass of champagne in a to-go coffee cup then another which is filled with sliced strawberries and a dash of salt.

The brush of the wind begins to really pick up. I see her figure shiver slightly.

I reach into the confines of the fabric tote, pulling out a fleece blanket that she can wrap herself in.

Annoyance floods her voice, "It is too cold for this. You should have picked another day to do this."

I release a slight laugh, "I am sorry."

She peers down at the drink, "We are not supposed to be doing this here, you know."

The weight of my head falls forward, "I know, I like the risk. So, there is something I want to talk to you about."

Her words are sharp, "What is it?"

The weight of her energy feels like it is crushing my chest, "I want us to be on the same page. I want us to have the best relationship ever. I want us to talk more. About how we feel and what is going to happen in our relationship. I feel like I am in the dark and It just—"

The sound of my voice becomes drowned out by her phone ringing.

The vibrations of her voice raise, "I am sorry. I have to take this. It is my boss."

A wave of sadness washes over me as I watch her walk away, 'Well, that did not go how I thought it would.'

Moments later she returns, placing her body next to me, leaving a good distance of separation between us, "So, what were you saying?"

The structure of my head pulls into a small shake, "Never mind. It does not matter."

Her tone jumps into the defense, "See! I do not know why you have so many questions? Why are you so needy for answers? Just let it be. Whatever will come of us, will. Look, I am not going to lie. I did not even think we would make it this far. So, when you ask me stuff like that, I do not have an answer. I do not think about stuff like that. Is what we have just not enough for you?"

My head bows slightly, not being fully sure how to respond or what to do from here.

The silence is broken by her emotionless tone, "You really have gotten the worst of me."

Her eyes fall towards the grassy structure of the ground, "Anyway, are you ready to go? I have stuff that I need to get done."

I can feel my mind attempting to retain all the information, but it leaves me unable to find my voice.

All I can do is nod my head as I think, 'I feel more confused than ever. Maybe, I am nothing to her, but a 'right now'. Maybe, that is all I will ever be.'

CHAPTER THIRTY-SIX:

I wake up on the morning of April second, something immediately feels wrong inside of my mind.

My brain appears to be in a rapid cycle of thoughts that surround Victoria, 'What if she is just like all of your exes? She has said things that they have in the same context, yet she is kind moments later. She leaves me feeling more unsure of my placement in her life every day. Some days, I feel like I am the best thing in the world to her others I feel like nothing more than a friend and then there are ones where it seems like I do not matter at all. What if she really does not love me? She says she does, but the way she acts, it leaves me with questions.

Sometimes, the things she says to me, it really hurts, but I try to find reasons, if she won't tell me then I have to find out in my own way. Just like the other day, on my birthday, she made a harsh comment, 'It is not like I did not have six months to plan it.'

Then the very next minute she will do something nice like buy me a pajama set for no reason or tell me that I am the only person she wants to spend the rest of her life with. I am just—lost.'

I like to call these things, 'triggers' I never know when one is going to happen, but when they happen without an understandable cause my mind begins to kick into paranoia. These thoughts, they consume me with negativity and falsified delusion. They leave me in a state of fear until I no longer have control. I have to tell her how I feel.'

I take a deep breath, seeing that in our most recent messages, the last one I sent, expressed my love for her in a lengthy note. Her typical response of three, red hearts is now showing it has been read by me.

I push my fingers to type a new topic.

Hey. Something you said the other day really got to me. You always tell me to tell you when something is not okay with me. I told you how I felt about your boss, I told you that it bothered me. I have been asking you to go have a drink with me, you said that you were to tired, but you could have gone with your boss. I said I would be patient being your secret, with your job, but I do not want to be half-loved. I feel like we are not in a relationship, I feel like we are in an agreement. You said, I am easy to cheat on, you said I am too nice, you said that I need to love myself more. I do love myself, I love myself a lot. But I love you, too. If you are not serious about me then why did you get my hopes up that you were? I would do anything for you, but I won' t stay where I do not feel wanted.

The weight of her reply comes back faster than before.

What are you talking about? I am so confused.

I find myself trying to figure out where I went wrong in my expression that she is confused.

My phone alerts me that she is trying to call, I ignore the attempts. I do not feel okay enough to speak on the phone.

Another text shoots in.

Why don' t you answer your damn phone?

The overpowering sensation of breaking down nudges against my mind.

I am sorry, but I can' t do this.

Tears stream down my face as I speak to myself in a cracking tone, "She really didn't love me. All she did was get upset."

Through blurred eyes, I block her from being able to get a hold of me for a while, just until I can sort my thoughts. I need to figure this out, now I cannot lose her.

CHAPTER THIRTY-SEVEN:

I feel the wind inside of the apartment beginning to increase as if the air conditioning is working on hyper-speed.

A sharp pain radiates throughout the center of my chest causing me to drop against my knees. My head falls backwards, tension lines my neck as I scream out in severe agony.

The next thing I feel is my body slamming against the floor of my apartment. It feels like all of the air has been knocked out of my lungs. My blurry vision scans the area, finding that I am in my house. Only, something about it now feels different.

The bones in my spine crack under the movements of me, pulling myself up into a full stance. I tilt my head to the left, seeing that there are twelve, bright yellow papers that are trying to push themselves inside through the framework of the entrance.

I rush to the door with a quiet, unsure stride, freeing one from the frame. My eyes widen as I realize it is an eviction notice—they all are. According to the dates, I have not paid rent in six months.

I know something is not right, my shaken form thumbs through my phone as I try to call Alex. The dial rings two times before a frantic voice fills the line, "Sam! Where the hell have you been? Everyone has been looking for you!"

The shock lining my mouth deepens as my eyes drift towards the leather book on the table, *'Holy shit. That was real.'*

The static bark of his tone causes my thoughts to break, "Dude! Hello?"

I stammer over my words, "I—I am sorry. I need you to get over here, now."

He laughs forcefully, "I have practically been living outside of your house. I have been so worried about you. If you came back, I wanted to be the first to know. I am at the door."

I hear the echo of his voice in the hallway, prompting me to end the call. The crack of the panel being released from the seal pops to life.

I watch the papers fall towards the ground in an effortless sway. He steps into the threshold, scanning me sharply as if trying to reason with his brain if I am real or not.

His concern shifts to rage, "Where were you?"

I gulp, looking towards the book, "You would not believe me, even if I told you."

His eyebrows raise slightly, "Look, I do not really care where you were. You just better have been writing."

My voice shakes in uncertainty, "I have."

A grim smile rides against his mouth, "Great. I'd love to see it."

I know I need to get the journal I have been working on, but I left it in the book. The weight of my thoughts causes my vision to become pinned against it.

He follows my gaze, "Oh, I see. Is it in here?"

I want to scream out *no,* but my voice fails to appear.

He tilts his head, examining the cover as *Fate* runs through his mind, "Ha, fate. What kind of name is that? You want to talk about fate, take it up with me. I am the one who covered your rent while you were off doing God, only knows what. That is fate."

His raging moods no longer phase me, "Alex, calm down. Thank you for helping me. Look, some guy gave me this book. When I write inside of this book, everything around me changes. And—"

Alex cuts me off, throwing his hands into the air, "Wait. Wait. Wait. Who did you say gave you this book? And, where did you meet them? That sounds like a pretty good story, right there."

A sudden knock at the door causes both of us to freeze. I cautiously approach the door.

The barrier reveals a familiar man, "Steve. Hey, what are you doing here?"

He allows himself to enter the house nodding towards Alex.

My face contours slightly, "Did you follow me home the other night?"

Steve flashes me a fast smile, "No, I was not following you. I was chasing after the book."

Alex raises his eyebrows sarcastically, "Oh! So, you are the guy who gave Sam the book. Great, this all makes sense now!"

I shake my head slowly, "Okay. Look, I do not know what you want from me, but if you look around at all the collections on the ground. I do not have any money."

His voice stiffens sharply, "I do not want your money."

Alex rolls his head back slowly, "Then what do you want? We were having a very important conversation when you interrupted it."

Steve has no intention of leaving anytime soon, he sits in the chair next to Alex, "I need Sam to talk to me."

The weight of my head tilts to the right, "About what?"

The tips of his fingers run against the leather binding, "You have to go back."

Alex sighs, "Oh, I get it! Is this one of your little friends you met while you were on your vacation?"

A deep sigh is extracted from my chest, "Alex, I was not on vacation. I was in this book."

The weight of his bottom lip drops down slightly, "Okay. Okay, I see what is going on here Sam. You are messed up in the head. It is all the damn liquor you're drinking. It's screwing you up, man."

I watch him walk towards the door, the fading call of his voice surrounds me, "Get the book done."

The harsh blow of the door slamming shut causes my body to jolt.

Steve's voice breaks into the air, "You are not messed up."

I drop my vision towards the book, "Who are you? And, what the hell is going on?"

Steve pulls his chair closer to the one Alex just left.

His right hand gently pats the empty cushion, "Sit."

A long, exhausted sigh leaves my throat, "Okay. I want answers, now."

I see his figure tense slightly, "What you are experiencing right now is a major life lesson. For you and Victoria. I hope you guys are paying attention."

The whites of my eyes appear brighter from my shock, "Right and you are, what? Are you trying to tell me that you think you are God?"

A deep laugh fills the area, "No, but having me here should be just as scary. Now, I need you to go back into the book and make up with Victoria."

All of the air is sucked out of my lungs, "She does not love me."

The weight of his head falls to the right, "How do you know that she does not love you?"

My vision squints sharply, "What do you mean?"

His shoulders shrug gently, "I mean, did she tell you, *I don't love you?*"

I exhale deeply, "No, but sometimes her actions make me think otherwise."

He pushes his lips together in a thinking manner, "Maybe, it has nothing to do with you at all. Maybe, this is something you should talk to her about."

The structure of my arms line against my chest, "I tried to tell her and she never gives me a real answer."

Our conversation is drowned out by the sound of the front cover of the book opening, releasing the looped version of Victoria's voice, "You are an asshole! My car broke down! Of all the days for you to do this to me!"

My vision dances towards Steve, "Yeah, that sure makes me want to go back."

He steps in my way as I try to escape down the hall, "Sam, this is not a joke. Victoria is your fate. Even if you do not believe anything else, believe that."

Again, the book begins to crack and bubble to life, speaking in the voice of my angel, "Sam. Babe, please, talk to me. I miss you. I do not know what I did wrong. Please, just meet me in person so we can talk about this. I do not want to lose you."

My vision turns to Steve for an answer, he pushes his head towards the book.

I take a deep breath, "Okay, but only because I love her."

The weight of my words hangs heavily in the airs before turning into artifacts of the book, pulling me in as well.

CHAPTER THIRTY-EIGHT:

This time the book drops me off in Victoria's world at my own house.

The second my feet hit the ground, I look down at my phone, finding that it is now April fifth.

I quickly head out the front door, getting Victoria on the line, "Hey. It is me."

I can hear the relief in her voice, "Hi. I did not want to miss your call. I have had my phone on loud just in case you called."

I nod my head once, "Meet me for coffee. I will be there in fifteen minutes."

Her voice trails from my mind as a tear falls down my face, 'I cannot believe I am about to see her again. I missed her so much.'

I find myself sitting in the outdoor patio section of the shop, awaiting her arrival. Finally, she pulls into view. We give each other a hug once she is out of the car then we find a place to sit. To neither of our surprise, we do not order a coffee.

I can feel the intensity of her anger, "Why did you do that to me? Huh? Why?"

My vision moves towards the table, "I got scared. I did not know what else to do. I tried to tell you how I felt all this time, but it just seemed like you did not care."

Her arms raise slightly, "When did you tell me this? I don't remember!"

The vibration of my tongue stiffens, "I told you a lot."

Her eyes roll up slightly, "If you did. It was vague, so vague I did not understand what you were trying to say. You need to learn how to communicate with me."

I shift my posture slightly, "I did not mean to confuse you. I wanted to understand what was going on between us, but it was impossible to figure anything out with not having good communication in our relationship."

The light in her eyes begins to slowly start fading, "You know what? No. I am so pissed off at you, right now. You left me. I had no way of contacting you."

The air inside of my chest becomes stuck, "I am sorry."

Her anger pulls her to the sturdy foundation of her feet as she starts walking towards the exit, "Goodbye."

My body does not jump to follow.

When she does not see my shadow in tail, she comes back to the table and sits down, "Look, I think a lot of this has to do with the fact that you are very young."

My throat barks in defense, "This has nothing to do with my age. It has to do with us not having a great structure for our relationship, but that is okay. It is something that can be fixed."

Her mind shifts to a different topic, "I love you."

My head tilts to the left, "I want us to be together. We just have to talk to each other more. We have to let each other in. We both need to fight for this."

She nods her head in agreement as I walk her to the car, "Thank you for coming."

Her eyes meet mine, "Thank you for calling."

She leaves me with the stained shade of her gloss against my lips.

I watch her car pull out of the parking lot, 'I really hope that we are able to get on the same page. Life without her, it just is not really a life at all. She brings something into my life, I think it is a good thing. It is just hard to explain. All I know is—I need her.'

CHAPTER THIRTY-NINE:

A few days later she held an event, sort of like the one we went to back in October, only this one is smaller. It is being personally held at someone's home and Victoria sent me the address an hour ago with a time to arrive.

My anxious mind pulls up to the side of the house at 7:59 p.m. giving me one minute to spare. I cannot convince my feet to move out of the cabin.

I quickly text her.

Hey, I am here. I am sitting in the car. My anxiety is so high I cannot walk to the door.

With no reply coming anywhere in sight, I exhale deeply, closing my eyes, wondering how I am ever going to get through this. All of the sudden, I hear a soft knock against the passenger side window.

It is Victoria smiling at me, "I wanted to come get you, since your anxiety is so bad. Are you okay?"

A deep breath of relief flashes over me, 'Thank God, she got there when she did.'

See, this is what I mean. She does things, things that make me fall deeper in love with her every day.

A few calendar days have passed us by now and with the seasons changing at a rapid pace, the darkened mass of clouds above act as a strong reminder.

My leg is being shocked by the phone vibrations from an incoming call.

It is Victoria, her tone is shifting between different vocal pitches, "Hey. I am on my way to my Mom's house. My Dad had to go to the hospital. He was throwing up really bad all night. My Mom had to call nine-one-one. I am on my way to get her then we are going to the hospital after."

My voice cracks against the stale air that surrounds me, "Please, keep me updated. I am here if you need anything."

I find myself waiting by the phone, just in case she needs me. I soon realize that it is driving me crazy to the point of mindlessly looking every fifteen minutes.

I exhale loudly, with the frustration I have in myself for stressing so much.

The loud ping of an incoming text pulls at my mind.

Hey. My Dad is stable. They are going to transfer him into ICU tomorrow. They think he had a stroke.

My thumbs tap against the screen in a rapid pace.

I am so sorry. Is he going to be okay?

I do not have to wait long for her response.

I do not know, yet. It is a waiting game.

The muscles lining my forearm strain as I push send.

Do you or your Mom need anything?

Before I have a chance to shut the application, another ding ignites the air.

Not yet, but I will.

I feel the weight of my mind, drifting towards Victoria, 'I wish there was something I could to do assist her. I feel so horrible that she is going through this. I do not understand fully, but I know enough that it breaks my heart for her and her family.'

Her Father has been in ICU for a few days now. It does not take much to see why her and her Mother do not want to leave his side.

In the meantime, I have been trying to help Victoria out the best I can. With me taking her youngest daughter to school it gives her a minute to breathe, I feel like it is not enough. I always ask her if she needs help, I want to do more, but at the same time I feel like she does not want it. I have been trying to assist her with making dinner as well. I do not know if I am doing a good job, but I want to make her life easier.

I suddenly become distracted by a text, it is from her.

Will you come keep me company at the hospital?

My eyes drift to the corner of my screen seeing that it is eleven at night.

Yes. I am on my way. Call when I get there.

My foot hardly hits the brake the entire drive. Now, that the vehicle is in park, I hit the dial.

The static rings three times before I get an answer, "Hey, I am in the waiting room of ICU."

I breath roughly around the word, "Okay."

The service clicks off as I enter the elevator. My eyes have a hard time adjusting to the soft lights, making my way through the maze of hospital furniture sprawled around in a reckless manner. I find her wrapped up in one of her sweaters.

I greet her with a growing grin, "Are you okay?"

She nods twice, using the back of her hands to wipe her eyes.

The weight of my head falls to the left in concern, "Do you need anything?"

Her vision drops, "No. Just having you here is enough. Thank you."

I attempt to relax on the uncomfortable chair next to her.

Once I feel settled, Victoria's words rattle through my mind, "Actually, I do need something. Could you go around the corner towards the bathrooms. You will see an open cabinet, inside is some pillows and stuff. Will you bring me one and also a blanket?"

The structure of her form expands into a full stance. It takes me longer than expected to retrieve the items. I quickly round the corner of the wall that is separating us, to see that she is trying to rearrange the furniture to make a bed area.

A small smirk rises to my face as I hand her the needed items and help in getting her more comfortable. I sit myself down in the lone chair beside her.

She turns her head in my direction, straining her neck, "We will wake up in a few hours to trade places with my Mom, so she can get some rest as well."

I nod my head firmly in a drowsy understanding.

The faint whisper of hope leaves her lips, "Good night."

I allow the figure of my left hand to rest against her back while she sleeps.

The sound of her and her Mother having a conversation knocks me back to reality. I immediately search the screen of my phone, learning that it is now one in the morning.

We sit in the dark, musty ICU room. My heart aches for Victoria and her family. The sleepless bug has also stung her Mom, who is already insisting that we switch places again and it is only three. She hardly got any sleep, but I guess, who would in her situation.

Once I am sure that Victoria is asleep. I run home to take a fast shower. On my way back to the hospital an hour later, I stop by the store to grab some toiletries. I hope it will give them a sense of normalcy.

I glance over at Victoria's exhausted form allowing my palm to embrace the back of her hand.

She slowly pulls her arm away from my reach, annoyance floods her tone, "You are always so close to me. Like, whoa. Back up."

I open my mouth trying to explain my concern, but my thoughts are never revealed. I take a deep breath, letting the thoughts go from my mind.

I get up to use the bathroom and the next thing I know I am in the cafeteria. I ran into her mom, who sent me on the search to find her something to eat. While I am in the area, I gather some stuff for Victoria as well.

Now, that they are going to be dealing with friends and family coming in for visitation, I think it is my cue to leave. Once out of the hospital, I head off to get some stuff done she needed help with, that I promised her I would take care of. I do not want her to stress over things that she does not have to right now. With me being away from reach, we are forced to communicate my text.

I ignite our conversation into a new topic.

Hey. I know that you have so much going on right now. It must be hard to even think. I just want you to know that I am here, if any of you need something. I am so blessed to have you in my life. I never want to be with anyone but you.

The notification pops up faster than what I am used to.

You know that I do not believe you, right? I cannot trust anything you say after you left me like that. You are going to have to earn my trust back. What? Did you think that you could just do something like that and it would all be forgotten? I do not know if I will ever fully trust you again. I used to think that you were a good person, but now that you did this, it put you back a few notches on that list.

I read the message twice, before putting the phone down in the cart. I want to give myself a moment to sort my thoughts before I reply in regret. I find myself, again trying to process her emotions.

While I finish up the few errands that needed to be done, I take time to type a reply.

I was not trying to hurt you. I panicked. When I thought that you did not love me. I thought that I tried hard to understand. I see now that I did not do enough. Again, I am so sorry.

Her thoughts translate to the screen quickly.

Are you ever going to do it again?

My mind explodes with emotion as I scan the inner confines of my brain.

I would not have left the first time, if I felt loved. Let me ask you again, why I would stay where I did not feel wanted?

I find myself waiting for a response that does not come. We end up ignoring the question and continue with a new day.

CHAPTER FORTY:

The rest of the week is spent at the hospital with Victoria. Many sleepless nights allow us to have more time to talk. I did not want to leave her there, even for a second. Just the thought of going home to my bed, knowing that she was not in hers, makes me sick to my stomach. Finally, her Dad has been announced as being stable enough to be moved into a rehab to assist in his recovery process.

Twenty days later, he is being sent home. Still not fully back to normal, but at least he gets to be in the comfort of his own environment. They have to have medical equipment delivered to the residence as well as a care giver to aid her Mother with his needs. Victoria finds herself spending as much time as she can helping out her Mother.

The vibration of my phone going off startles me, "Hello?"

Victoria's voice blares through my mind, "My car broke down and it is in the shop being fixed right now. I do not have a car and I am not sure when I will get it back. Can you come get me and take me to my Mom's house?"

I confirm with her that I will be there in ten minutes before hanging up the line and walking out the door. She swears that going to a tanning bed makes her feel a hundred times better. We stop by the local gym as well as a small, off-brand market to get things for her Mother before making it to the destination.

Once we arrive at her childhood home. I jump out of the car, once given the okay to get out, to help her carry things in. I leave the vehicle in the driveway, not knowing how long I am going to stay. Family members and friends of her father's begin showing up to the house to see him. They block my car into the driveway.

Victoria notices this before me, she flashes me a fast grin, "I am sorry that you are now stuck here for a while."

I shake my head slightly, "There is no where I would rather be 'stuck' than with you."

We begin doing things to help her parents around the house. Since, we are currently outside on the patio swing, we start around the external chores.

My vision melts over her, "I think I found a house to rent."

Her attention remains focused on the bushes, "Oh, really? Where is it at?"

My mind holds steady on my hands which are hard at work, "Waterway drive. It is just down the street from your house."

Her silence causes me to look in her direction, searching for an answer in her body language. The focal point of her glare falls heavily against me.

I can sense the rage that is now radiating along her form, "No. That is not okay."

At first, I assume she is going to crack a smile, telling me that it was a joke. Unfortunately, that is not the case. I can feel myself searching her eyes, but all I find is more anger.

My voice cracks in uncertainty, "You are kidding, right?"

Her eyes widen as she takes a step closer to me, "No. I do not want you that close to me. No. Find somewhere else to live."

I can feel the weight of my head shake slightly, "Okay."

The rest of the night, something was off about us. We should have been talking a lot more than we did.

Her emotional tension hangs over me on my ride home, 'Okay, that was weird. Why does she not want me there? It would be great. If she would just look at it from my point of view, we could be closer, I could help her more with her tasks and I could give her way more affection. Yet, she reacted so badly. I do not get it. I mean, I could understand if we had only been together a few weeks then I spring something like that on her, but we have been together now for nearly a year. At this point in most relationships, this is where they figure out if they want to move to the next step of their agreement. Most of the time, this involves living together. Yet, she does not even want me to be two blocks down the street. I do not know what she is doing or thinking, but right now with that last spat, she really has me thinking, does she truly love me?'

These same thoughts keep multiplying and getting stronger throughout the next few days.

Finally, three days later, I send her a text.

I hoped that I was missing something in this situation and wanted to know if my theory about her is correct, that she just got overwhelmed by the idea.

The structure of my thumbs begins to compose a message.

Hey, the other day when I told you about the house. Were you serious?

Her response comes through roughly an hour later.

About what? You not living there? Yes, I was serious.

A deep exhale leaves my throat.

I do not understand why you do not want me there. What do you think I am going to do? Stalk you?

The quickness of her reply catches my interest, being out of her normal behavior.

Yes.

Two more thoughts drive into my inbox over the next few seconds.

No. Idk.

The humidity in my breath lines the display screen with fog.

I am not going to stalk you. I just think that it is weird. You never want to talk to me about a future together then me moving two blocks away from you freaks you out. What do you want me to think? That everything is normal and okay? It really feels like you are either trying to hide me or hide from me. I cannot tell which one.

The blare of her ring tone blocks out the surrounding noise.

My eyes jolt around as the word cracks with uncertainty, "Hello?"

The strained tension of her voice raids my mind, "You know that I have a fear of people following me. I told you, I am really paranoid. I am sorry, I do not have an answer for it. All I can say is that I just do not like it. I do not want you that close."

My silence only causes her irritation to grow larger.

A fast breath of air is pushed out of her throat, "Anyway, what are you doing?"

The stress in my shoulders tighten, "I am going to go eat some seafood. What are you doing?"

An exhausted moan fills the line, "I am helping my Mom out right now then I am going to go home and try to get some rest. Who are you going to eat with?"

My head shakes as if she were in front of me, "No one."

A shift in her voice causes her words to become high pitched, "You are going to go eat dinner by yourself?"

The small glimpse of a smile rises to my mouth, "Yeah, I do it all the time. It is no big deal babe. I promise."

A touch of disapproval is found in her voice, "Why didn't you ask me to go with you to eat dinner?"

My shoulders drop slightly as if in defeat, "Every time I do ask, you say no."

She tries to validate her point, "You should still ask me. You never know if I will say yes."

The structure of my mind freezes against something she just said, my brain begins to feel like I am losing control of my own thoughts and feelings as my head explodes with thoughts, 'See, this is the kind of thing that makes me freak out. The way she says things, she makes it seem like I am nothing, but a game to her and that is the last thing I wanted her to think of me as.'

I release a loud groan, laying my face into the structure of my palms, 'I wish these thoughts would just leave me alone. I just want to be happy with Victoria. That is all I want, but having my thoughts creeping around in every shadow, makes it nearly impossible.'

The fight in my skull begins to slowly drift away from my reality as nothing more than just a way to blow off steam, when another thought echoes through the back of my mind, 'Or, maybe I am just still wishing and hoping that we will be able to make it through this, without losing each other along the way.

CHAPTER FORTY-ONE:

My mind has had me up all night, tossing and turning through thoughts as I attempt to gain control, but fail every time.

There is only one thing that my mind can agree on, 'I need to talk to Victoria. I have to get some answers. I need to understand this. She always tells me to meet her in person, if we need to talk about something important or serious. I think this is a point that would fall into both major categories.'

The positive guidance of my thoughts leads me to a small bar and grill that sits just down the block from my house. Once I place my order for the first drink of the day vodka and lemonade, I decide it's time to give her a call.

At first, she does not answer the ringer.

The weight of my shoulders shrugs slightly, "She is probably just sleeping. I got all day to drink, enjoy the weather and wait for her to call me back. No stress. I need to walk into this conversation in a relaxed, calm manner.'

Just as my mind starts to settle in a boat of peaceful thoughts, the sound of my phone breaks through the air, it is Victoria. To be honest, I would have been disappointed if it was anyone else trying to reach me.

My voice trembles slightly, "Hey."

A loud puff of air is pushed towards the speaker, "Sorry. I missed your call. What's up?"

The uncertainty of my mind causes me to stumble over my words, "Could you come up here to the grill and meet with me?"

Her irritation only grows stronger, "Meet you? Why?"

A line of strength fills my voice, "I wanted to talk to you."

She pushes a breath of annoyance into the speaker, "What do you want to talk about?"

The memory of a past conversation with her rushes through my mind, 'Please, promise me, you will see me in person if you have to talk to me about something important.'

A light chuckle leaves my throat, "No. It is okay. I just will wait until we can meet to talk."

Her words bite at my ear, "No. Tell me, now."

My mind begins to explode under the pressure. The words I wish would come to the surface, remain nothing more than a jumbled mess of thoughts and feelings in my chest.

Finally, the weight of my bottom lip falls, but nothing I crave comes out, "I am not happy. I feel like I am running in circles, but nothing is good enough for you—"

She releases a sigh of irritation, cutting off my words, "Okay, okay. Bye."

I hear the sound of the line running dead, alongside of my shattering heart, 'Does this mean that she does not love me? Does this mean that she is tired of me?'

Before my mind is able to fully get a grasp on what is happening. I feel the hard push of something unseen slamming into the center of my chest.

I tense my figure, knowing that another blow is not too far away. I notice the pressure of a hard, wooden object is now jabbing into my back.

I exhale loudly, looking around to see that the same waitress is now standing beside me, with a look of concern flooding her face, "Do you want another drink?"

A falsified grin attempts to fill the blank look on my face, "Keep them coming."

With my mind running at a million miles an hour, I shift my attention towards my phone trying to speed up the text I am writing to Alex.

Hey.

I am at the grill. Will you come up here and meet with me? Victoria and I are having some problems.

I allow the screen of my device to turn black, laying it face up, hoping to get a fast reply.

It does not take long before the blur of something crosses my vision from the right side of me.

My brain begins to pulse trying to put information to the shadow, it is Alex.

He slides into the chair across from me, "What is going on, now?"

His vision scans me quickly, "You look like shit."

I release a deep breath, placing the weight of my head against my palms.

Alex throws his head in every direction, speaking in a strained tone, "Where is the waitress?"

I offer no help, shrugging my shoulders gently.

The loudness of his voice causes my figure to jump, "I want the same thing as my saddened friend over here."

A slight pause forms in his words, turning the direction of his facial canvas towards me, "Sam, do you want another drink?"

The structure of my head falls forward as I whisper, "Yes."

I feel that her presence has left the table, my vision stays held into a locked position against the light washed wood of the structure.

Alex shifts his body slightly trying to piece together what to say to me, "Look, I am sorry for how I acted last time we spoke. I did a lot of thinking about my actions and I realize now that I handled the situation wrong. I do not know whether I believe what you are telling me, but I am willing to trust you in order to find out. If not—I am asking you to promise me, you will get help after all of this is over."

I allow nothing, besides the hot breath of fire to escape my lungs in his direction.

His eyes dart towards the ground behind me, speaking in a fast, irrational tone, "Let me help, now. What can I do?"

I run the surface of my interior hand down the front of my face in annoyance, "Well, first of all, I want her. I do not want to lose this girl, Alex. This is not a joke, I need you to take this seriously. She is the one. I just have to figure out why she does not love me, but I can't even figure out my own thoughts, nevertheless hers. That is what I should do first."

The drinks are now arriving at the table, pulling Alex's mind in for the first sip, "Okay. So, what is the plan?"

My head tilts to the right sharply, "What plan? There is no plan. This was not what was supposed to happen! We were just going to sit down and work through our issues. Then the next thing I know, she hangs up on me like I am nothing and now, I do not know what to do."

He puts both of his palms towards me in a defensive manner, "Hey, knock it off. Calm down, we will figure this out. You said earlier that before you talk to her, you want to figure out what is going on inside of that head of yours, right?"

The weight of my skull moves forward slightly, "Yes. I want to be able to sit down and be able to explain everything to her in an organized, clean manner. I want us to be able to lay all of our selves down on the table and make sure that we are on the same page."

Alex breathes roughly into the glass causing the inside to fog up momentarily, "Okay. What do we have to do next then? You are the boss. She is your girl, you call the shots. I am just here to help out when I can."

The structure of my eyes rolls in an upwards sway, "Why are you doing all of this to help me?"

His vision darts to the side of the table, refraining from eye contact, "I need you to finish that book you are supposed to be writing."

He pauses softly, "And, because you are my friend. This girl seems to make you really happy and I only want what is best for you."

CHAPTER FORTY-TWO:

Later that night I find myself with mounds of paperwork and blank, manila envelopes flooding the ground around my apartment.

We are currently on our third pot of coffee, with sleep being the furthest thing from my mind.

I figured that I might find it easier to sort my thoughts if I make them into a real object, that I can touch and feel. Each envelope has a category title such as: I love you, reasons to stay together, reasons to break up, etc.

Alex looks around the room as he sighs, "Come on, dude. Can we not just make this easier by dealing with one topic at a time?"

A slight chuckle exits my throat, "No can do. I am sorry, man, but my mind does not work like that. I just write down what comes to my head. Each piece of paper has its own thought. All you have to do is file it into the correct folder. It is not that hard, Alex."

His head rolls back slightly fueled by irritation, "Do you have any idea how long this is going to take? You know what sounds like a simpler plan, calling her on the phone."

I breathe deeply at his sarcastic comment, "I do not want to talk to her, until I know for a fact that my thoughts are in order."

Alex stands sharply, waving his open palms towards the carpet, "Look around, these are all of your thoughts. They might not be organized, but they are here. She can look through them at her own pace then get back to you once she processes the information."

The structure of my lips presses together tightly in a thinking manner, "I guess, that could work. Okay, let's do that."

Alex claps his hands together sharply, "How are we going to do this? Go to her house or what?"

My mind begins to spin under the question, "Uh—no. Shit. That is one of the major problems here. I cannot go to her house. What if she is not home and one of the kids answer? She will think I am stalking her."

Alex runs his right hand through the strands of his hair in a restless manner, "Okay. Well, why don't you put it in a big envelope with her name on it and leave it on her porch?"

My eyes squint sharply in his direction, "Again, like I said, if her kids get any kind of indication that I am trying to win back their mom. I lose any chance we have at a relationship. Everything we have worked for would just go down the drain. We have done everything possible to keep this relationship a secret, I cannot destroy that now. I cannot destroy her. We are trying to fix this, not make it worse."

He swallows sharply, "Okay. Where would we be able to find her then?"

I release a long gust of air, "There is only one place she might be, but it is a long shot."

He steps closer to me in excitement, "Great! Where is it?"

I speak softly, hoping to keep the word hidden under my breath, "Dallas."

His eyes widen sharply, "Dallas? You are telling me that we are going to drive all the way to Dallas to walk the streets looking for her? Are you crazy?"

My sweaty palms tighten their grip around the stack of papers, "Only about her. Come on, let's go."

I allow the entire weight of the information from my brain to be held in my left hand while I reach for the keys using the right.

My head turns slightly towards him, "Grab the book."

Once we are both in the car, I scan him softly, ensuring the book is in fact present.

His voice fills the cabin with a curious tone, "Where are we going?"

I breath roughly through the crack in my lips, "Dallas."

The structure of his brows caves slightly, "Yes, in the book. Why are we going to Dallas in our world? We should be trying to get there in hers and the gateway there you said is in this book."

Irritation begins to flood my words, "I learned that when I enter or leave the book, it will sometimes send me to the same part of hers that I was in while being part of ours. So, it will either take us to Dallas or it won't, but I think it is worth a shot."

Red splotches of shock litter along his face, "Wait, we are doing all of this on a maybe? And, hey what happens if when we try to come back, we get dropped off somewhere in our world other than Dallas without a car?"

I nod slightly allowing all of his concerns to be properly placed away in my mind, "What better things do you have to do anyway tonight?"

His silence sets the mood for the rest of the drive.

Once we arrive, he seems to have a peppier atmosphere surrounding him, "Okay. So, now we are going to do what? Put the book down and just jump inside?"

I shake my head in a fast, twitching motion to his lack of knowledge, "No. All I have to do is put the book down in an open position somewhere in the car and talk."

The look of doubt on his face becomes more visible now that I have given him the instructions. He does not allow the emotion to wipe from his face the entire time that I am setting up.

I release a strong gust of air from the chambers of my lungs, "Okay, Alex and I are about to re-enter the book. Hopefully, we will be able to find Victoria."

His pupils begin to enlarge slightly, reflecting the image of the words that left my mouth, that are now hanging above our heads in a shredded paper formation.

They travel at a fast, spiraling pace towards the binding of the pages, the currents are so intense they pull us inside as well.

We find ourselves roaming the dark streets, without a single place that we have to be. We search the area for miles in every direction. Looking high and low. We blend into the crowds that cover the city streets in masses to the highest points that are made available. We scan every face, hoping to find her among the nameless bystanders. During the course of the next five days, I find myself jumping in and out of the book, hoping to catch even the slightest glimpse of hope that she is out there somewhere, looking for me as well. All I find is people who resembled her.

I begin to feel completely defeated. All this time I spent looking for her and she never even tried to contact me once.

My brain begins to jump to the worst end, 'I guess, this is the answer I have been looking for. Maybe, she does not want me to find her.'

I take a deep breath allowing my mind to become one with the ink allowing it to scratch me out of the next scene and back into the hands of my reality.

Alex becomes engulfed in a coughing fit as he feels his body ram into the uncomfortable passenger seat of my car.

He speaks in a broken tone, "What the hell just happened?"

I use my right hand to start the vehicle, "We are not in the book anymore. We are going home. We did not find her. We did not even come close and you know what the funniest part is? I do not even know what I would do if I saw her, right now. Even though I have been doing nothing, but wishing to find her. I do not even know what I would say to her if she was standing in front of me. I have wasted all of my time trying to find her instead of working on myself. If I did talk to her right now, we both know it would be a disaster and I only get one chance. I cannot mess it up."

He nods his head once in a hopeful understanding.

My mind begins to travel out into the vast space that surrounds me as I try to think of new ways to get this information across properly.

Alex does not mind my silence, he is wrapped inside the peaceful melody that is rolling through the cabin. It dances along the current of the open windows and into the light of the stars that hang above.

When I get home, I am completely exhausted. Not even the thought of coffee or vodka is enough to awaken my soul.

The flashing clock on my phone informs me that it is only ten-thirty at night.

I throw my clothed figure onto the couch in a careless manner, but something in my mind will not allow me to find mental peace.

The chaos roaming the halls of my brain begin to crave the calming effects of nicotine.

I groan in irritation, pulling my sleepy form towards the patio door. The burning flame holds my attention, until a familiar vehicle pulls down the parking lot in my direction from the right.

My mind whispers softly, *'It is Victoria.'*

I shake my head in sheer disbelief, *'There is no way that she would ever come up here. There is no way that she would ever come out of her world. This is insane. she is not real.'*

The shaken tone of anger flies around me, "I want you to talk to my daughter, she's in the car."

My mind switches to a state of confusion, *'Why did she bring her daughter here? Did she somehow find out about us?'*

With the thoughts of the entire world now feeling like they are suffocating me, I can do nothing other than panic.

My distracting brain pulls me away from reality and further into my mind. The sounds of her walking towards me causes the breath to catch inside of my throat.

She speaks in a now, softer tone, reaching her arms out to me, "Come here. Let me hold you."

The pull of my aching heart wants to do nothing in this moment other than run to her arms, the only place I have ever felt at home.

My mind releases a fire of thoughts, stopping me from pouring her in a shower of love, *'She does not love you.'*

I gulp slightly, realizing that my heart is going to start fighting back, *'Then why is she here? If she is in front of me then she loves me, right?'*

My brain releases a harsh laugh, *'You know what she is doing. You have seen this before with your exes. They would leave or treat you bad then they would try to get you back, just to do it again. Like it was some kind of sick game.'*

The vibrations in my heart string to life, *'She is different. You love her and you know she loves you, too. Just relax, it will all be okay.'*

Without saying a word to Victoria, I hurry into the house. I leave the door cracked slightly, wanting her to know that I will be right back.

I can see the look of confusion on her face, reflecting in the moon lit patio glass, *'I feel so guilty, but I cannot seem to find my voice to explain the feelings that are racing through every inch of my soul.'*

Through the maze of thoughts, somehow I still manage to be able to find my phone in the dimly lit room and dial Alex's number with trembling thumbs.

The shot of her voice is filled with anger, it hits me as soon as I step back out onto the concrete slab outside my side door, "Who are you calling?"

I begin to feel the pressure of her question, closing in around me. Still, my voice is nowhere to be found.

He answers with a voice filled of concern, picking up on the third ring, "Hey, Sam. What's up?"

I quickly scan my memories, thinking back to the time he told me a code word to use if I am in trouble.

I stumble over my tongue, "I need your help, she is here."

It is as if I can see the confusion melting on his face through the phone, "What? What do you mean, *she is there?*"

My pupils dance inside of their sockets, "I do not know. Just come here, okay?"

The weight of the phone is quickly transported into my pocket as I throw my body over the four-foot-tall, iron railing that is currently separating us. I release my grip on the chipping, black, top bar, the moment my feet come in contact with the ground.

We are now face to face, my eyes catch a fast glimpse of hers, '*I love her so much. There is nothing more that I want than to be able to wrap my arms around her and kiss her so deeply that, it would almost seem like none of this ever happened, but I cannot. We have to talk first. I have to tell her how I feel. I just need more time to think, but I—*'

My thoughts are shattered by Victoria, calling after me.

I allow the chaos in my mind to pull me further away from where she parked, "Hey! Where are you going?"

I turn my attention automatically onto the vehicle she arrived in.

I cannot see her daughter in the car, but I do see the dome light on, with the drivers side door left wide open, '*Victoria, I am not running away from you. If your daughter really is in that car, we cannot talk properly in front of it.*'

Victoria whispers to me sharply, "What is going on?"

I lick my lips slightly, "I just want to talk to you."

Her body moves at me in a fast motion, "About what?"

I shoot my vision towards the cement, "Us. Why did you tell me that I was easy to cheat on? Why do you not need me? I need you! Why don't you—"

The trail of my vocal cords are shattered, "I do want you! I want you! Is that not enough for you?"

CHAPTER FORTY-THREE:

I release a deep buildup of air, "No. I want you to need me."

Her attention falls in a downwards angle, "Do you want me to leave?"

The weight of my head shakes roughly in confusion, "What? No."

The focus of my body turns in the other direction. She wastes no time jumping in my way trying to wrap herself around me.

I pull away slightly, knowing that if I allow her to embrace me, I will completely fall apart.

I can already feel the tears stinging the back of my eyes, *'I cannot hug you. I will collapse. I need to be strong right now, babe. I need to understand what is going on, so I do not lose you.'*

My voice shakes, "What can I do?"

The currents of my mind scream, *'Why did you say that!? Out of all of the things that decide to come out of your mouth, why that?'*

She exhales slightly, "I want closure."

I feel the weight of my mind beginning to crush me, *'This is not good. She wants to do the same thing as what my exes did. She is trying to make me feel like I am confused. I do not know what to do. If I give her closure that means that we are really over and that is the one thing I am not going to let happen.'*

My head shakes slightly, "No. I am not going to do that. I am sorry."

She replies in a harsh growl, "Why?"

My anxiety makes her voice sound like it is amplified.

Slowly fading from my mind causing me to trip over my words, "I think you are manipulating me."

Immediately, I realize what I have done, *'I have made a mistake. I should not have said anything! Where is Alex? He is supposed to be here to help me out right now.'*

My brain is locked inside such a mess all I can do is start walking, hoping that it will make things clearer.

Victoria's voice scrapes against my ears, "Should I be scared of whoever this person is that you called? Are they coming to beat me up?"

I cannot help but to let out a small, nervous laugh, "What? No. I would never hurt you. They are coming here for me, not for you."

Her head tilts to the left slightly, "Do you want me to leave?"

I blurt out my response roughly, "No."

A flash of yellow light surrounds us, the beams from Alex's car are extremely bright in the dead of night. He pulls into the spot, not even getting a full chance to place the vehicle in park. I waste no time, hoping into the cabin.

My tone shakes, "I do not know how she got here, but her daughter is here, too. We can talk about that later. Right now, I need you to distract her while I attempt to organize my thoughts."

He nods once, turning all his focus onto Victoria, who is now walking up the front side of the car towards his window.

The weight of his left, index finger opens it slowly, "Hi."

She leans her body against the car's frame, "I am not talking to you, Alex. I am speaking to Sam."

The structure of my head leans towards her, "Yes?"

Her left eye twitches sharply, "I cannot believe out of all people you call him. I thought that you said he was a jerk, an asshole, that you and he have not been friends for a while."

Alex nods his head slightly, "We did have some issues, but we figured that we could try to work them all out."

Her eyes burn against me, "You are sick. Do you know that? You are sick in the head and you need help!"

The weight of my head falls backwards slightly, '*I know I do, but we can talk about that at another time.*'

Again, her voice pounds against my figure, "This is why I do not want to be with you."

My vision squints sharply, "Then why are you here? If you do not want to be with me? I am not sick, it is something else."

Her posture shifts without warning to a harsher demeanor, "I loved you, that is why. Who ever said that you were sick?"

My vision is pushed tightly together by my confused brow, "You did? Five minute ago. You just said you *loved* me, earlier when you got here you said that you still do. See, this is what I mean, you say one thing one minute then something else the very next. I never know what to think or what is true."

Alex uses his head to draw all of the attention onto himself, "Wait. You loved Sam? Like past tense? You do not love Sam, now?"

My mind explodes in fear with his comment, '*Alex, shut up. What are you doing?*'

These actions cause a nervous laugh to slip out past my throat.

She shifts her weight to her left leg in irritation, "No. I still love Sam."

He overpowers her tone, "Then why did you say that Sam was sick?"

Her eyes widen sharply, "I never said that. Sam does this all the time. You change things that I say and make it seem horrible. I never said that you were sick or that I did not love you."

I am unable to do anything in the moment, other than hopelessly watch her walk towards her car.

The weight of my form sinks into the seat as tears streams down my face, "Now, what am I going to do? I cannot lose her, Alex. I need her. Tell me what I am supposed to do now. Why do I mess up the one thing I only want to be perfect? Her. Help me. Please, I am begging you. I cannot lose her."

I finally make my way into the house after watching her disappear from my view. I use my right hand to punch the panel of my front door as I walk in. I am so numb to the pain, due to the exhaustion in my heart. I did not sleep all night, my mind kept playing the scene of my horrid attempt to fix our relationship.

Finally, it is four in the morning an appropriate time to be awake. I hurry to the kitchen to start my first pot of coffee for the day. While that is perking, I head out to the patio to get a quick buzz. I watch the paper slowly burn as I think about the work event I have later today.

The book signing lasted a lot longer than I expected. I am just now dragging myself into the front door at three in the afternoon. Something hanging on the door catches my attention. It is a letter from Victoria.

My heart begins to pound erratically as I struggle to unfold the three pages which are written upon torn out sections in a black inked, cursive scroll,

Sam,

I am sorry. I was a total failure as your girlfriend. I never gave you the love nor the time you wanted. I got so involved with the shit in my head that I got lost in my own struggles and shut you out. I shut everyone out. I hate myself for being that way, for being this way. I am my worst enemy. Be forever mad at me. You deserve better than me, I have always said that and thinking back, I always felt in my heart that you would leave me. Perhaps, my subconscious always kept my feelings for you controlled because I was scared of getting hurt. I was always afraid of our differences, I did not want you to leave me because your life is taking off. You are going places, you are somebody. On the other hand, I am now at a point in my life, where I want to settle down and share my life with someone that wants the same thing.

I know I pushed you away and if I did not look for you any sooner, it is only because I know this is best for you.

You do not need me. One day, you will have a young and beautiful girl by your side and she will make you very happy.

Thank you for loving me when you did. Believe me, I still love you with all of my heart and soul. Hard for you to believe, but it is true. I want you to know I did need you (I do).

I have missed you like crazy. I wish I could make love to you, I wish I could give you all of those hugs and kisses you always asked for. If I had another chance, I would do everything differently. I would not hold back and I would show you what I really feel without fear. I always did say, you got the worst of me. You came into my life when everything was falling apart, everything is broke, I am broken and even more now. I should have truly fought hard for you. It will be something I will live with every day. I deserve it though, I deserve it. I have so much regret, I need you and I want you like crazy. I do not want to ever hurt you again.

Do not ever forget that I love you. I fucked up. If you ever find it in your heart to give me another chance, I am here. I wish I could see you, I wish I could make love to you and give you everything you want. I would put my heart on the line and risk my all, for one last time. One last time. One last chance. If only, I can swallow my pride and do what it takes to win you over. I do not want to move on without you. See me one last time.

*I am not your exes. I do not collect people. I just simply want to be with you. *

Victoria.

P. S.

I love you. I need you! I want you. I promise things will be different. I will fight for you, for us. I am just afraid you will put a restraining order on me if I keep looking for you. Please do not.

I miss you, if it is really over—ugh. I am going crazy without you. Let me love you. Your call, your terms, just let me love you like I never got to materialize my love for you.

Let me do that, now. Let me be who I am with you.

I wish I could see you.

I find myself reading the letter multiple times, feeling a little confused, *'In the beginning of the note, she said things that are making me feel like she does not want to be with me, but the rest of the message appeared to be informing me that she does. I just—I need to see her in person.'*

I feel the weight of my body bounce around the room as my mind screams out in joy, *'Yes! Yes! There is hope! I have to go find her, right now!'*

The plastered smile on my face begins to melt as my right palm clasps around the doorknob, *'Wait, I have to figure out what is going on inside of my mind first.'*

The rest of the day I find myself being completely emerged in my thoughts. It does not take long for the sinking sun to shine rays of light into my eyes from the next day's burning hues.

The strong pound of a knock upon the door, draws my attention away from my thoughts. My steps are quick and filled with annoyance at whoever this is that is interrupting my process. I pull the door towards myself, the dark reflection of my eyes shows that it is Steve, who is standing on the other side of the door. His facial structure creates a fake smile causing him to look more frightening than helpful.

My lungs release a deep breath of air, "What do you want?"

He tilts his head to the right, "Why are you mad at me? I am not the one who messed up your relationship. I am only trying to help and I could help you through this if you allow me to."

The weight of my arms fling over the structure of my chest, "Fine. You want to help? My mind is a mess. Can you fix that?"

The roughness of my tone surprises me, nearly making me fall backwards from shock.

My face softens slightly as he shakes his head, "No, but I can assist you in doing it for yourself. Okay so, all you have to do is listen to what I have to say then ponder on it for a while. Okay? She is your fate, Sam. There is nothing that you can do to change that. Your feelings for her are only going to grow stronger with each day that passes. The two of you just have to decide if you want the time to pass with good memories or bad. Either way, time is going to pass you both. Do not miss out on the time you have together right now because you will never get that time back again. You love her and she loves you, this crap needs to stop. Now, get your head together and go find her. She misses you, just as much as you miss her."

Steve allows the tone of his voice to echo through the hallway as he stares at me in silence, waiting for my mind to connect the wires of information he has just given me.

I nod my head once, speaking in a fast tone, "Okay, got it. Thanks."

The weight of the door begins to be pushed forwards by my right arm as I create a barrier between me and Steve. He puts his left arm in the direction of the frame and the wooden panel, stopping it from fully closing.

I release a loud puff of air, "What?"

He looks around the area with concerned eyes, "I have to tell you something else."

My shoulders stiffen under the idea of him staying any longer, "What? You said that after the first thing you wanted to tell me that you would go away for right now. It is not personal, I really appreciate everything you have done for me, but I need time right now to think everything through. My mind is just as messy as my life and I do not need any added stress right now. You can understand that, right? Great. Thanks, bye."

I hear the seal of the door finally be closed between us. I use my right, index finger and thumb to quickly ensure that the conversation is going to stay over by locking the top bolt.

I take a deep inhale of air, feeling like I can finally breath again now that I am alone with my thoughts.

I turn around to feel the fear of seeing Steve standing behind me, his tone is released in a casual sway, "You thought you could get away from me that easily? Please. Come on now. I told you that we needed to talk and I meant that. Now, about Victoria. What are you trying to accomplish here? Do you want her to come back and you guys deal with your past or do you get back together and only look ahead at the future and start fresh every day?"

The weight of my head falls to the left as I am wrapped inside my own mind for way longer than I would like to admit, "I want us to completely start over. There is nothing we can do to change what happened between us. No matter how much we fight, we cry, we laugh, it will never change the hurt we already put on each other. The only thing we can do from here is take every new day for what it is worth."

Steve nods his head slowly, looking down at the bracelet Victoria gave me on my arm, "You are going to have to pack all of those things away from your relationship before this happened if you guys want to have a good future. Personal items like this, they end up holding onto your energy. You know how powerful energy is Sam, you write about helping people and giving them the best ways to live their lives. It is about time you start taking your own advice. I am tired of seeing you make everyone else's life better, it is time to fix your own. Get your stuff together before you not only lose her, but also yourself."

I nod my head once, he shows himself to the door not long after we finish our conversation that ends in a thick silence hanging over us.

With me now being alone in my thoughts, I am able to process everything with a clearer mind after taking Steve's advice on helping myself first.

I feel the weight of tears running down the sides of my face as I place our items into a box. The tension in my heart is beginning to make me want to stop, but I know that he is right and that it will make our relationship stronger. Maybe, one day we can bring them out again, but for right now, we need to focus on the future.

I exhale sharply allowing my body to collapse against the legs of the couch, *'Finally, I feel like I can get what I need to say across to her.'*

CHAPTER FORTY-FOUR:

The shaky form of my right hand reaches for the phone as I type a note to Victoria.

Hey, meet me at Northeast community park, off of blue mound rd. I will be sitting at a picnic table. It is eleven, right now. I will be there until noon.

I take a deep breath, pushing all of my weight into the book with a small, stepping motion on the top of the table.

The overpowering sound of the wind whistling through my ears as I travel to Victoria's world is amazing.

I find that the book has allowed me the gift of not having to travel too far, making sure that I am in the correct spot.

I do not get a response from Victoria, but it does not wavier my mood. I attempt to stay as calm as possible, hoping that nothing will affect our energy.

It is hard for me not to continuously look down at my phone screen, watching the time stretch closer to twelve o'clock. Still, no word from her.

I sigh gently as the digits shift from 11:59 a.m. to 12:00 p.m.

Yet, I still find myself unable to move, knowing that she will be in contact soon. I breathe deeply allowing my thoughts to drift towards the time. I see that it is now 12:58 p.m.

The sound of an incoming voice mail catches my interest, 'I did not even hear my phone ring. This is weird.'

The weight of the phone now lays in my hand as I scroll through the messages, until finally, I find the one that is from Victoria, "Hey. Sorry I did not see your message until now. I had intentionally left my phone downstairs, I kept looking at it. Waiting and waiting for you to call. Please, call me back soon."

The weight of my eyes close in relief as I dial up the number.

Her voice cracks through the speaker, "Hello?"

My eyes begin to tear up slightly, I try to keep the emotions from overflowing into my tone, "Hey. Do you still want to meet up with me?"

It seems like the words cannot escape her mouth fast enough, "Yes. Where are you?"

I inhale sharply, "Still at the park."

An urgency begins to run through her words, "Okay. I will be right there."

The sound of the phone call ending, triggers my mind to release a stream of pain, 'Thank you, God. Thank you. I cannot lose her. Thank you.'

I wander over to my vehicle, a small storm has been brewing in the sky. I do not want her to have to sit outside in it with me.

Minutes passing feels like an eternity to me as my mind tries to process the amount of time it would take her to get here. The melody of the raindrops slamming against the windshield guides my thoughts.

Finally, I can hear the sound of incoming tires gliding against the gravel road.

I can feel the rapid pound of my heart beating faster into my inner chest with excitement. I waste no time, jumping out of the car. She does the same, embracing me into a hug.

All the stress in my figure vanishes with her now being wrapped tightly in my grasp.

She releases me gently, "Do you want to sit in the car and talk?"

Even though it has now stopped raining, the confines of the vehicle gives us more privacy. I nod my head once in a silent reply, making my way over towards the passenger side.

The eerie dullness inside of the cabin consumes us. She begins to shift in her seat, letting the front part of her form face towards me.

The soft flow of her white dress, covered in yellow petaled flowers catches my eye, 'She is so beautiful.'

Her voice comes to life, "I am sorry that I was not a good girlfriend. I went to the doctor and they helped me. I finally have answers to why I am the way I am and I can start getting help."

I allow the weight of my head to fall into my palms as I lean forward trying to ease my mind from the heavy downpour of guilt that surrounds me, 'I wish I would have known. I had no idea that something was wrong. I thought you just did not love me. I feel so bad. I do not know how to fix it.'

She speaks in a comforting tone, "Can I touch you?"

I push my head in a forward manner, not being able to find any more strength in my voice.

The gentle touch of her right hand, running along the structure of my back sends shivers down my leg. She entangles her fingertips along the strands of my hair allowing me to melt completely into her affection.

I turn my body towards her without warning, I lean in for a kiss. She does not hesitate to mimic my movements, the brush of her lips against mine, taste like water after I have been stranded in the desert for years.

She breathes into my mouth, "I want to kiss you. I want to make love to you. I want to hold you. I want to be with you. I want to do life with you."

The emotions pour from my lips in a delicate sway, "Me too. That is all I want is you. That is it—just me and you."

A gigantic smile runs against the surface of her mouth, "I am taking off work tomorrow. I want to spend the entire day with you."

My eyes squint sharply in confusion, "You do not have to do that."

The weight of her head tilts to the right, "No. I know, I do not have to. I want to spend the day with you. We will start off with coffee and go from there. I will pick you up in the morning."

A sigh of relief leaves a humid mist to glaze my bottom lip, "Sounds great. I cannot wait."

She smiles towards me, "I have to go now. I was leaving to go somewhere else when you called. You caught me as I was walking out of the door, but I will message you throughout the night."

I nod in understanding. The gentle kiss of our love is shared before I get out of her car and into my own.

The drive home from the park for me is filled with drops of gratefulness as I thank God for letting us still remain together.

A few hours pass, when I receive the first message from her.

I cannot wait to see you tomorrow! I love you very much!

I smirk gently to myself as I reply.

Me either, I am excited! I love you, angel.

CHAPTER FORTY-FIVE:

The next morning, I find myself awake a lot sooner than normal, but I cannot help it. I am so anxious to see her in a little bit, my mind can do nothing other than think about how much I love her.

I have been fully dressed and ready to go since six o'clock this morning. It is currently nine fifty-eight and I am beginning to feel quite restless.

Suddenly, I hear the sound I have been waiting for to break against the air currents.

My mind reels as I speak in an uplifted voice on the phone, "Good morning, beautiful."

A light laugh slips out of her throat, "Good morning, my love. I am on my way to your house. I will be there in a minute."

The next thing I know, I am grabbing my keys and rushing out the door. I am so ecstatic, nothing else is able to be fully processed in my mind.

The weight of my figure slides into the seat, where I am greeted by the gorgeous smile of my wonderful girlfriend.

We start out our day by going to the tailor. She needs some adjustments made to articles of clothing. Three dresses and a skirt make up the small fashion show I am given while they determine how they need to be aligned.

Once the agreements are finalized, we head over to a large, food-chain cafe to get a bite to eat.

After we have finished our coffee and food items, she clears her throat, "So, what do you want to do today?"

A spark in my eye ignites under the thought spiraling through my mind, "Can we jump on the train and go to Dallas?"

She tilts her head slightly, "You want to take the train?"

A small chuckle slips out of my lips, glaring down at the half-eaten plate of destroyed hash browns, "Yes. We can walk around or have a drink and just talk."

She thinks over the information in her mind, "Okay. We can do that, it sounds great. Are you ready to go?"

I nod once and we head to the train station. The entire ride, we find ourselves roaming from car to car in search of a bathroom. Finally, it is found and we jump off after the next stop.

We begin wandering the nearby streets in search of a comfortable place to sit. A nearby Mexican restaurant with an outdoor patio becomes our temporary home for the course of the next few hours.

We have just finished ordering our drinks when the conversation turn serious.

She swallows roughly, "I want to understand what happened a few days ago."

My eyes glance softly to the side, "I was confused. I panicked, I thought that you did not love me. I thought that you did not want to be with me and I did not know what to do."

She tilts her head to the left slowly, examining me, "I told you all the time that I loved you. I might not have been there all the time or given you all of my love, but I did the best I could under the circumstances of how I felt. I guess, it just was not enough for you."

The tone of my words become stale under the pain I feel in my heart from her assuming her love is not enough for me, "It was not the things you did not do that made me worry. It was the things that you did do, that made me panic."

It is clear that the information greets her with shock, "Explain."

I exhale a deep breath, knowing that this is going to be a length paragraph, "You said, I was easy to cheat on. I was easy to take advantage of because I am too nice. That you would never need me. You tell me I cannot live by you and you get all upset with me for suggesting it. You tell me to communicate better with you, but when I try to talk about it or ask you questions, you either ignore it completely or tell me that we can talk about it later yet, we never do.

It just made me feel like you did not care about me or my feelings. Then the day I called, I was not breaking up with you. Technically, no one broke up with anyone. You just hung up on me and I thought that it was your way of telling me, 'screw you'. I did not know what to think or what to feel.

After so much time of me asking you for answers and receiving none, it left me with no other option than to make my own assumptions. I just needed time to process what exactly was going on.'

She nods her head slowly in deep thought, "I am sorry if I made you feel that way. After that happened, I went to the doctor. Finally, receiving an answer to why I felt so bad this whole time. Now, that I am on medication and I know what I am fighting. I feel better. I no longer seem numb to life.

I want to make love to you, kiss you, hold you, spend time with you because I can actually feel now.

After I took the medication, it made me start thinking. It made me realize just how much I love you. How much I miss you. It made me realize that I do need you. I want you and I want to do life with you, only you."

I feel the burn of an uncontrollable smile run along my face, "I want all of that as well. With you, only you. I am sorry that it happened."

She shakes her head gently, "It is weird how it played out. You got upset, I went to the doctor, then I had this realization. Almost, like it was meant to happen this way."

She sighs gently, her eyes are searching my face as she drops her attention towards the legs of the table, "Things make more sense to me now of why I was the way I was. The reason I never told you how I felt about you was because even though. I knew that I loved you, I could not make the words come out of me and replay them to you.

You are able to write me novels about how you feel about me, but I cannot even organize my thoughts, I will try to be better at that. Sometimes when you ask me a lot of questions or send me long messages, it becomes overwhelming for me and I cannot process the information, nor do I know how to reply. That is why I send you the three heart symbols. That is my way of telling you, 'I love you, too.'

I was not able to give you my time because I always felt numb to the rest of the world, it was never that I did not want to spend time with you. It was that my illness made me be unable to. Sometimes even something as simple as returning a text or a phone call felt like it was just too much.

Also, I am not a big fan of public displays of affection, I never did that before. It was not because I did not want to be with you or did not love you.

There are so many other things that make so much sense to me now and I want you to know, so you can better understand how my brain works and that way if these things ever happen again, you will know why. Instead of thinking that I just do not love you because that is not the case."

I feel a weight lift from my chest as her voice begins to fade into my mind, "Everything is so different now. Thank you for telling me. I *feel like I can finally understand what is going on. See, this is all I was looking for the entire time. Reasons. It not only will give me peace of mind, but it will also help me love you better and be more understanding to things. Thank you for sharing this. I am not worried about this anymore. If we would have had this conversation before that phone call, none of this would have ever happened.*

I would never feel like you do not care or love me ever, again because now I understand where you are coming from with your responses or actions. See, this is why communication is so important. I am glad that we were able to do this today. I wish we could have done it a lot sooner. It would have saved a lot of pain for both of us."

Her voice trails behind mine in a soft manner, *"There is nothing we can do to change what happened in the past. We can only look ahead and work on the future together."*

We share the delicate communication of a smile.

Suddenly, her face shifts slightly, *"Are you ready to head back to Fort Worth? I have some stuff that I need to do yet tonight."*

The next thing I know, we are on the train heading home. It took us no time at all to find our seats on the upper level of the transportation system and get settled.

She reaches for my hand while laying her head against mine.

My mind begins to reel with emotions, *'She normally pulls away from me when I try to show her any affection in a public setting. For her to initiate this, makes my heart overflow with love under the warming sensation of her touch.'*

The rest of the week goes great. We find time to see each other as much as possible.

Communication appears to be a lot smoother between us now. I finally feel like we are on the same page and that we are going to be *just fine from here on out. The thought in itself is strong enough to give me a lifetime of peace.*

She is making me feel loved, secure and wanted. Everything that I craved the last eight months. I become so overjoyed, I do not know how to handle any of my emotions.

The ping of an incoming text piques my interest. At the same moment I hear a knock against the front door.

My mind begins to scan the words of the information sent to me by Victoria as I slowly creep towards the front door.

I think this is all a really good thing. We can use this opportunity to get a fresh start from here and have the best life together.

I can no longer hold the grin from breaking free of my internal persona.

The weight of the door swings in my direction causing the muscles in my mouth to drop, seeing that it is Steve, "What are you doing here? How did you get into the book?"

His relaxed posture does not become phased by my irrational mind as his body leans against the door frame, "I told you. I am an angel. I can go anywhere and do anything, but I am here because I want to talk to you about something."

A serious vibe crashes into the room as he steps over the threshold without asking to be granted permission, finding a place to sit on the couch.

He exhales deeply, wasting no time to get to the point, "The battle with Victoria getting better is not over. Those pills are not magic, you two still have a long way to go, but you are on the right path. Not to mention, the idea of a new beginning is not going to happen—"

Fear shoots through my form, "It is not? Why not?"

The punch of my anger causes his head to tip back slightly, "Hold on, calm down. You did not let me finish. It is not going to happen unless you go and get help as well. You have been through so much in your life, Sam. It is time to leave that part of you behind. That way, you can have a great life with her. She is trying to be the best version of herself for you. You have to do the same thing for her. Remember, how bad it made you feel when it seemed like you were the only one fighting for your relationship? Do not make her feel like that, now."

His words have a massive effect on my mind, "You are right. I want to be the best partner for her. I have to do this. Thank you."

We are now starting the second week of our new relationship. I have a doctor appointment next week on Wednesday. We cannot wait for them to be able to tell me what is going on and how they are going to help me. I am beyond excited to feel better. I know that it gives Victoria a sense of peace as well.

I have noticed that she seems to be having a good reaction to the treatment they are providing for her. So far, we are still doing great with communication. The time we spend together is much deeper in a connection than ever before, I have never felt so loved by anyone in my entire life as I have for the past two weeks.

I am so thankful for her. I am glad to see that she is beginning to feel better and be happy, I know no one who deserves it more than her.

The phone begins to ring, my mind glances towards the message from Victoria.

I was actually thinking, my youngest daughter will probably only be here for four more years. Maybe, at that time we can talk about possibly living together. Even if no one knows yet at that time that we are dating then we will just *tell people that you are my best friend and we are roommates.*

I feel the weight of my bottom lip drape down slightly, 'This is the first time she has ever talk about a future with me.'

I close my eyes allowing the currents of my mind to carry me into a dream-like state, where I can see my entire life with her playing out like a movie.

The next morning, I awake to it being Friday, June twenty-first. I have an event today from three to nine p.m. I do not want to go, the only desire I have is to spend time with Victoria.

She has a follow up doctor appointment today which is a good thing. Even though she has been feeling better, there are still some concerns she has about certain 'glitches'.

A few hours have passed, when I get a call from her.

She speaks in an upbeat tone, "They gave me another medication to add to the others. They think this one will really help me."

My head bobs along to the melody of her voice, "Good. I am happy to hear this. When are you going to start taking it?"

Her response is uplifted, "Right away. I want to know if it is going to make me feel better or not."

I swallow hard, "Good, you will have to let me know."

Her mind remains hopeful, "I will. I am on the way to my Mom's house right now. I wish I was with you. I hope you have fun at your event. I will talk to you later. I love you."

I speak through a growing smile, "I cannot wait to talk later. I love you."

The hours seem like they are crawling by. Finally, my interest is piqued by the scream of my phone being bombarded with texts from Victoria.

Babe. This medication is the best thing ever! I feel so much better, it seems like everything is so clear now and my mind is very organized!

I wish I would have done this a long time ago.

Babe. I love you.

I love you.

I only want a life with you.

I miss you.

My eyes widen slightly as I release a small laugh to myself, 'I have never seen her like this. I love it. I am glad she is feeling better.'

My thumbs react to the desire to give her my full attention.

Good! I am so happy that you are feeling better. I love you, baby.

Her response is insanely fast from what I am used to.

Am I being too much?

A fading smile flashes along my lips.

No, you are not. In fact, I love it.

Just as the message sends, anther one comes through my device.

Good.

CHAPTER FORTY-SIX:

She has been on the new medication now for four days. The second day, I was hoping to be greeted with the same, bubbly spirit that was there yesterday, but that is not the case.

Her voice seems heavy when she answers the phone, it is the first time I have heard this kind of emotion from her in almost two weeks.

It instantly raises my concern, "Hey, babe. How are you feeling today?"

She sighs deeply, "I am okay. Yeah, I am okay. I just have a lot on my mind. I thought that I was going to feel like I did yesterday, but I do not."

The structure of my lips push together in a thinking manner, "Maybe, they need to lower the dosage or up it."

Her reply is delayed slightly, "Yeah, maybe. I will bring it up to the doctor when I see them next."

I nod my head gently, almost as if I am forgetting that she cannot see me.

The next day arrives faster than I thought it would. I get to spend the majority of the day with Victoria at an event for her passion. She picks me up around one thirty in the afternoon. The moment I get into her vehicle I can sense that her mood has yet to bounce back.

I try to hide the worry, but it is visible in my vision, "Are you okay?"

She nods her head once as if thinking over a fast response, "Yeah, I will be okay. Maybe, the medication just needs some time to kick in fully. Today will be a really big test. If I am able to sit still for the entire two hours without fidgeting then that is a really good sign."

The event went really well, Victoria seems much happier than the last time we were here. And on a plus side, she hardly became restless at all. Yet, her overall mood does seem to be going in a negative angle more every day. I cannot figure it out exactly, but something just seems very off.

Over the course of the next two days, irritation would appear to be overtaking her form. We have been fighting a lot lately. I promised her that I would keep an eye on the symptoms, but yet asking her makes me feel guilty. I do not want her to take it the wrong way, I just care.

I allow a deep intake of air to flood my body with relaxation as I type.

Are you doing your night work?

The response is fast.

I should be, but no. I am too exhausted. My phone is about to cut out.

My vision squints sharply.

Your phone is about to cut out?

Her thumbs type a steady stream of her thoughts.

Why can' t I see your icon in the chat? And, my phone is going to die.

A small laugh crawls up the back of my throat.

Why don' t you get your charger, silly?

Her *mind is on a different topic.*

I do not like that I can' t see it. Can you see mine?

My fingers translate my answer slowly.

Yes.

The *next piece of information that rolls in on the screen is a shot of her trying to make me understand why she is frustrated.*

My brain scans the picture, looking for anything that is out of the ordinary.

A possible explanation flows through my mind.

Oh, you cannot see me typing?

I can feel her tension through the next set of messages,

No. That is not what I mean. Ugh. Never mind.

The *small amount of liquid in my mouth is pushed roughly down my throat.*

Do you think that the new medication is helping?

Her *mind sends back a spiral of emotion.*

Why are you asking? Bc I feel funky? I do not know.

I exhale loudly at the screen, trying to ease the anxiety in my mind.

Yes. Just checking in on you.

The reply takes a moment to be seen.

I am fine. I am actually going to put myself to bed now. I think I need to end this day with sleep.

CHAPTER FORTY-SEVEN:

I take a deep breath, finding myself sitting in the waiting area of a psychiatrist's office in Plano. The area is small, but that is not what gets to me. It is the blank, white walls, the cold, metal chairs and the sleepy receptionist that makes me feel like I have already been found insane.

My arms are still vibrating from the tension in my white knuckled grip along the steering wheel on the ride here which took nearly an hour and a half. The structure of my right leg begins to bounce trying to mimic the rhythm of the clock on the wall to my right. It is driving me crazy.

I release a deep breath as a woman calls through the glass window, "Gollakner."

Upon standing to my feet, I scan the vacant room and laugh slightly to myself at the irony that these people think I am the crazy one.

The woman does not want her identity to be seen by me as she walks at a fast pace in front, leaving at least two feet of separation between our figures.

The sound of her pastel, pink scrubs swishing together as she walks causes my jaw to tighten in irritation.

Loose strands of her fading, blonde hair dance along the surface of her paled neck. Using only her left arm as guidance, she points into one of the rooms. Silently instructing me to enter.

I follow the orders with caution, not knowing what to expect next.

A wave of relief washes against me, finding nothing besides a woman, a dark stained office desk and two chairs, that look like they were pulled out of a Victorian style home.

The woman meets me halfway in advancement, extending out her right hand to shake mine, "Hello. You must be Sam. I am April. Please, have a seat."

I give no answer as a reply, I quickly lower my body into the uncomfortable, leather seat which is stained light brown in color. It is supported by a thin wooden frame.

Her smile begins to fade, "Okay, Sam. We will start off with an easy one. What happened to get you here, into my office today? I have no idea what is going on. You are going to have to catch me up."

My vision drops, releasing a slow puff of air, "When I was nine, I watched my Father die. At twelve I was diagnosed with severe depression. I was given medication and was sent home. They tried every depression medicine possible but still, I had a bad reaction to every single one and— "

She squints sharply, "What was the reaction?"

I begin to squirm in my seat, "I wanted to kill myself with a smile on my face. I could not feel a thing. I could break my own bones and not flinch."

The structure of her brows raises, "Continue."

I sigh, feeling the dryness of my lungs, "At thirteen, when the depression medication did not work, I was diagnosed with severe anxiety. Now, on a cocktail of medication, the bad reaction only grew more intense and the suicide became almost an everyday attempt.

At fifteen, I was put in a mental hospital for two weeks, where they diagnosed me with Schizophrenia. They came to that conclusion because I have a gift of being able to see things that others cannot. I was released from the hospital, but I kept going to counselor after counselor and doctor after doctor for years trying to find an answer to why I am the way I am. Finally, I was sent here to you, being told I had been misdiagnosed my whole life."

She tilts her head to the right, "What do you mean when you said, 'Why I am like I am?'"

My shoulders tense under the question, "I just. I know something is wrong. I have known it for a very long time. I just do not know how to explain it."

A heavy silence falls around the room, before she pushes me further, "Can you try? It will help me to figure out how to help you."

I roll the weight of my head back slightly, crossing my arms over my chest, "Sometimes, I can eat decently, but most days I can go without eating a thing.

I am always restless, I cannot sit still. My legs and arms always feel like I want to rip them off of my body because they are so jittery.

If I am at an event or a party and it is indoors, I get anxiety really bad. I have to go outside and have a cigarette or go on a small walk just to feel like I can finally breath again. If the event is outside, I will feel better but still, it is a battle.

I have extreme sweating and a mind that always feels foggy, almost like I am living inside of a dream, only I cannot tell what parts are true or just my imagination.

I never know how I will wake up. Will I be irritated? Angry? Happy? Or, sad? I never know what it will be. You know how most people will wake up and are in a good mood, until something happens like spilling their coffee then that makes them angry? Not me, I do not need a reason. My emotions change randomly and once they do, I have no control of how long it will last or why it is there.

Other people have started to notice my symptoms. I no longer am good at hiding them like I once was. For example, I will be somewhere with people and I will be happy, outgoing, talkative then for no reason at all, I shut down. All my feelings fade and boom—everything changes. I stay for a while longer, if someone were to tell me a joke when I am in this state, I would laugh with everyone else because I know I am supposed to not because I actually feel the emotion. I always find myself looking at other people in envy of how happy they are, how easy their lives must be, wishing I felt, 'normal'.

At night, I feel like there are bugs crawling all over my body. I begin to freak out every time and turn on the light, but nothing is ever there. Sleeping is my best friend and my worst enemy. My anxiety keeps me awake most nights, but even on days where I can sleep, it never seems like it is enough. Sometimes my mental fatigue is so intense, I think that a whole twenty-four hours of rest would not be enough to heal my soul.

I always have to be fidgeting with something to keep my mind at bay. If not, I cannot get through most daily functions.

I have horrible memory loss. I cannot remember things, sometimes I will forget things that happened a few days ago. People tend to get frustrated with me when I do not remember or try to fill in the blanks myself and get the details wrong. They think I am being deceitful, but the truth is, I just cannot remember.

I am unable to perform at one hundred percent in any aspect of my life because my mind or body will not allow me to.

I have poor hygiene habits to the point, where I will get annoyed with myself, yet I am too exhausted to fix it. My life is as messy and unorganized as my mind, if that tells you anything at all.

I have a constant feeling of emptiness and a low self-esteem, that makes me feel like nobody will ever love me or want me. I even begin *to hate myself on days like that. Other days, I feel like the most confident being in the entire universe and that nothing can stop me. Neither of these things I have control of.*

I talk too fast. Sometimes, I even slur my words or speak in a way that does not even sound like English.

My palms are always cold and clammy, even if it is summer.

I tried to self-medicate for a long time, but it never affected me like it did everyone else. No matter how much I used or how much I drank, my demons still found me. Addiction was never a problem for me. I could quit any time and I did, when it was found to be useless to me.

I do impulsive things without reason, sometimes self-destructive things or take risks, most people would not.

I constantly want to run away. To where? That's the weird part, I do not know where. I just want to run. I have no inner peace and a hard time making decisions.

I hear things that no one else can hear like, loud ringing or a static radio. I am so extremely paranoid. Every time I leave my house, I fear that someone is following me or is out to get me. When I am in my house, I feel like someone has cameras hidden in the vents in my house as well as on my laptop and television. Sometimes, the fear is so intense I refrain from going into certain rooms or using devices.

I have questioned my own sanity many times. Yet, I am never sure whether I am insane or not."

By the look on the doctor's face, I can tell that she knows what is wrong with me which is a huge relief, to know that I am finally going to get an answer.

She prescribes me an anti-psychotic medication alongside a therapy plan, "All the symptoms that you were explaining to me earlier will go away once you start taking the medicine. I am sorry that it took the medical field so long to get you help."

I nod once to her in approval. I feel like my legs cannot move fast enough as I rush out of the building and to my car. I cannot wait to get started on this new path of my life with Victoria.

I place the dial to my right ear trying to slow my breathing. On the third ring I am greeted by her soft tone, "Hello?"

I smile widely, hoping that I am strong enough to restrain my emotions from overflowing into my words, "Hi, babe. They were finally able to give me an answer. Everything is going to be okay from here on out. We are going to be okay. I am so glad that I get to spend the rest of my life with you. Thank you for loving me, you are doing it perfectly."

CHAPTER FORTY-EIGHT:

The next morning, I awake with a different kind of light surrounding me. I feel my throat releasing a tune as I make coffee and take a drag from the cigarette hanging between my lips. No more than five minutes pass from me taking the first sip of coffee, I hear a knock upon the door.

My speed towards the barrier is fast as my curious mind needs answers to who could be here this early.

The new light that is breaking over the horizon, shows Steve. He greets me with a slight tip of his head and a widening smile. The structure of his legs carries him further inside with a careless stroll.

Confusion is drawn from my chest, lingering over my words, "Is everything okay?"

He flashes me a small grin, "Yes, everything is fine. I am glad you and Victoria are feeling better. I was getting kind of worried about the two of you there for a minute, but I never had any doubts that you would get through it together."

He breathes deeply, "I am here because you have to make a decision for both of you. That is, if you want to stay with her."

My mind begins to race as I cannot help but to blurt out, "Of course, I want to stay with her."

Steve uses his right palm to stroke the imaginary, facial hair on his chin in a downwards manner, "Well, then. I guess, I will just get straight to the point.

I need to know, do you want to stay here in the book as her secret or do you want her to come out into your world with you and lose her family and friends?"

My voice barely allows him to finish before I jump into the conversation.

I find myself speaking in a harsher than normal tone, "I will stay here with her. I do not want her to lose her friends and family. I would rather be her secret than force her to go through any kind of unnecessary emotional stress."

Steve tilts his head to the right slightly, "Are you sure? You do realize what you are agreeing to, right?

Sam, you will lose your friends, your life will only exist here, inside of her world. To everyone else in the universe you will never be anything more than just her best friend. Are you sure this is something you can handle?"

My bottom lip drops slightly as if I am about to speak.

Steve raises his right palm out towards me, "Shh. Do not tell me, tell her."

My vision squints in his direction with confusion. I follow the movement of his right, index finger which is extended out away from his form in the path of my hallway.

I step forward with my left leg holding all of the weight as I try to get a better view of what is he pointing at. My eyes explode with flakes of love as they rain down around Victoria. The weight of my eye lids slides down briefly, knocking me back into reality.

I begin feeling nervous, it stretches into my tone, "Hi, babe."

She lowers her gaze towards the messy strands of carpet, "Hi there. How are you?"

I look towards Steve as if he would have the answer. His brows squish together tightly, extending his hand in a waving motion towards her.

Nodding my head once in understanding with his silent form of communication.

An uneasy grin flashes towards her figure, "Phew. Okay, I have to tell you something. I am not very good at this, but it needs to be said. Here it goes."

I pause momentarily, hoping to gather enough courage to begin, "Victoria, I want to start by saying I love you.

I want you to know, I did not fall in love with you because of your body, your hair, your smile or your teeth.

I fell in love with you because the way your laugh makes every ounce of stress in my life magically melt away. I fell in love with the way your eyes captivate me more than anything because it is the closest view I will ever get to catching a glimpse of your soul. I fell in love with the way the sound of your voice can calm the darkest demons that live inside of my mind. I fell in love with you for all of the things that make you—you. I fell in love with the way you walk, the way you eat, how you love me and most importantly—with who you are.

I need you to know that when I am with you, it is not just for the good times, it is for the bad times, too. I know that we are never going to have a perfect relationship. This is not a fairy tale, trust me. I know, I write them for a living. All it is, is a reflection of what we as authors want love to be like, but in reality, that is not true. In the real world we have ups and downs and sometimes the downs become so much we want to panic and freak out on each other for no reason.

If we could just take the time out to understand one other, to be patient when days are hard. Because life will always be happening around us, there will never be a day where everything is perfect. There will always be something, even if it is not in our relationship, but no matter what happens, there is no one in this entire world that I would rather have by my side when my whole world is falling apart other than you. You are not just my girlfriend, Victoria. You are my best friend.

Look, what I am trying to say is no, our relationship is not perfect and it never will be. We have to stop aiming for perfection and start aiming for love. Because in this world the most amazing form of magic we have is love. It is beautiful, but real love is messy, it is a lot of understanding and patience, it is learning someone not as what we want them to be, but who they are and still choosing to love them, anyway.

You used to tell me that you thought love was a choice, not a feeling and I always said that I believed that as well. So, when we fight and break up, it hurts more because we know that it is not a feeling that is gone, but a choice to not love the other one. I want you to know that even if I had a million feelings of why we would not work, I will always chase the choice to love you because I know that regardless of what is thrown our way, we will come out stronger. I will continue to choose you for the rest of my life.

All I need to know is, are you willing to continue to choose me as well?

I know that since our journey has begun, it has not been an easy road to travel down, for either one of us. I know that we have had a lot of ups and downs. Emotionally, mentally, physically and financially, but I want you to know—there is not one person on this Earth that I would have rather gone through all of that with than you.

I would rather go through hard times every single day with you than be with someone else and go through nothing but good. I would rather fight every day with you and hear the vibrations of your voice screaming at me than kiss someone else. I would rather heal myself along the way with you while you heal yourself than be with someone who thinks they are perfect.

One of my favorite things about you is not only that you can admit when you do something wrong, but you also accept the fact that

I am just human as well and I will fail, but regardless of the downs, we always come back out on top, together.

I know that we have both done things that left the other one feeling confused, hurt or even ready to walk away from it all, but our love is so strong when we are together. It always will overcome every struggle that tries to get in our way.

I want to wake up every morning to the scenery of your body curled up in a messy fashion of left-over dreams. I want to fall asleep every night in your arms, the only place that I have ever truly felt at home.

I want to live inside of every frame of your life, things in this life mean nothing to me if I cannot share them with you.

I can't imagine talking to someone else on the phone, listening to them tell me about their day, when the only voice I want to start and end my day lives inside of you.

I can't drive in someone else's car while they place their right hand on my thigh and tell me that I am attractive because there is no one else in this world who can make me believe it like you do.

I can't even think of trying to convince my heart to attempt to love someone else, when my heart has already made up its mind, you are the only one it wants and it will not settle for anything less.

I can stay your secret. I do not care if we are the only two who knows as long as we stay loyal to each other that is all that matters.

I can do my best every day to try and make you see that you did the right thing by choosing me, I know that I can be everything you have ever wanted.

I can give you every ounce of love that I have inside of me because love is a choice and I want you to know in any life, in any version of realty, at any age, in any world, I would choose you a million times.

I need to be the greatest version of myself for you because you deserve nothing less than the best.

I need you and I do not need a lot of things, but baby I do need you."

Steve steps forward, waving his arms in irritation in front of his form, "Okay, come on, author. What are you going to do?"

I turn my head slightly towards Victoria, leaning in to share a kiss.

I can almost taste her along my tongue as I whisper into her mouth, "I need to stay here with you."

Well, maybe there is no such thing as a perfect woman, but there is such a thing as the perfect love.

THE END

Continue reading here…

CHAPTER FORTY-NINE:

Alex waits in the lobby of MVC Inc, knocking the sole of his left, black oxford against the maroon, tile floor.

A woman begins walking down the hall towards Alex.

He sharply throws his head towards the sound of her light gray, felt heels that are clicking against the glossy foundation. Her body is wrapped tightly in a matching pencil skirt, with a tucked in white, button down shirt. The entire outfit is held together with a coordinated blazer.

The red stained gloss on the surface of her lips stands out against her pale flesh, "Mr. Trier?"

Alex inhales sharply, mentally trying to prepare himself before following the messy strands of her light brown hair that are trying to sneak out of her bun as she walks. She leads him down the slim passageway, littered with different closed doors.

The weight of her figure stops at the two, main, glass panels at the far end, "Go ahead and go in. Mr. Vail is expecting you. Good Luck."

Alex nods once in a thankful manner to her. He uses his right palm to press against the door on the left side, nudging it open.

He is greeted by the walls being sheer glass, this takes him back slightly. He looks around the surroundings to find that the whole room from the ceiling to the gray carpet flooring, gives a gorgeous view of the Dallas skyline. There is not many pieces occupying the area. There is one, modern styled, black stained desk sitting in the center of the area. One, matching, leather guest chair and one, office version.

The work chair holds an older man, in his mid-sixties, he is currently staring out the window.

He speaks in a raspy tone, "Sam?"

Alex swallows hard, "No, sir. I am Alex. I am Sam's agent. I think we have spoken on the phone a few times."

Mr. Vail turns the chair around to face Alex, revealing sun kissed skin and gray hair cut in a clean style. He leaves his face clean and his bright green eyes appear to be rested.

A slight look of concern casts over him, "Well then, Alex. What is it that I can do for you?"

The man quickly raises his right, index finger causing the sleeve of his navy-blue blazer to sway in the air, "Wait. Before you answer that, I have a question for you. Where is Sam? The deadline on that next book is today at midnight."

Alex's eyes fill with knowledge, "Right, that is actually why I am here. Sam sends condolences about not being able to be here, but I was sent to drop off the manuscript in person. This is a very important piece of work."

Alex lays the manila folder down on the desk, it holds the ripped-out pages of the book inside. It is currently being slid closer to Mr. Vail by Alex.

The man tilts his head to the right, grabbing the item, "Is Sam going to come back any time soon? We have some things we need to discuss."

Alex feels heat rising to the structure of his cheek bones, "I am not sure, sir."

Mr. Vail nods his head in understanding, flipping the cover off the file open, revealing the cover page.

He squishes his vision, making it easier for him to see the letters while he reads the text out loud,

> *"Between the Pages.*
>
> *A novel.*
>
> *Written by:*
>
> *Samantha Gollakner."*

The man raises his eyebrows slightly, "For as long as I have known her, she still hates it when I call her Samantha."

Alex cannot help but laugh as he thinks back at how true that last statement is, "She does the same thing to me."

Mr. Vail nods twice, "Okay, Alex. Tell me, what is *Between the Pages* about?"

Alex feels the words beginning to stumble over his tongue, "It is a romance, sir. The synopsis is on the next page, if you want to read it."

He pushes his back into a straighter position before reading out loud the information on the next page, *"My name is Sam, I am a twenty-three-year-old Published Author. I am looking for something and we all know how hard it is to find the perfect woman, right?*

One night I found myself sitting in a bar, when a man walked in that changed my life forever.

He gave me an empty journal and told me to write about the girl of my dreams.

That night, in my drunken state, I decided to give it a try.

The next thing I know, here I am, writing my own love story, but there are a few twists. The woman of my dreams is forty-two and not only that, but she is also a single mother of three kids.

Come with us as we travel out of the world we know and into hers. It exists between the two covers of the book that you are currently holding in your hands.

Before we go any further, the first rule is, you have to keep quiet. Our relationship is a secret. Don't worry, you can stay. Just promise me you won't make a sound. Come on, we have to go find out if the perfect girl exists."

Mr. Vail looks up from the page, glancing towards Alex, "Where does she come up with all of these weird dream worlds?"

Alex tries to hold down a small, nervous laugh, "I do not know, sir. It almost seems like she lived it."

FOLLOW ME:

TWITTER @BOOKLIFEEEE
FACEBOOK @BOOKLIFEEE
INSTAGRAM @GOLLAKNERSAM
YOUTUBE@SAMANTHAGOLLAKNER
OFFICIAL

www.ingramcontent.com/pod-product-compliance
Lightning Source LLC
Chambersburg PA
CBHW022044240626
47154CB00007B/2561